CELG

THE SILVER TRAIL

Carter O'Brien's gun is for hire, but only when the job — and the money — is right. As tough as they come, he's been everything from lawman to bounty hunter in his time. Right now he's riding shotgun on an expedition led by an old Army buddy. The goal: to find a lost canyon of silver down in Mexico. But the way is blocked not only by gunmen working for a greedy businessman, but also a ghost from O'Brien's past.

BEN BRIDGES

THE
SILVER
TRAIL

Complete and Unabridged

LINFORD
Leicester

First published in Great Britain in 1986

First Linford Edition
published 2017

A catalogue record for this book is available
from the British Library.

ISBN 978–1–4448–3412–3

Published by
F. A. Thorpe (Publishing)
Anstey, Leicestershire

Set by Words & Graphics Ltd.
Anstey, Leicestershire
Printed and bound in Great Britain by
T. J. International Ltd., Padstow, Cornwall

This book is printed on acid-free paper

1

It was a mixture of business and pleasure that brought O'Brien to Tucson. The pleasure involved whiskey and the business was all to do with the man he had arranged to meet here on this sixteenth day of June, 1880.

At that time of evening the saloon was crowded and smoke hung around the lamps that studded the low ceiling in a misty shroud. O'Brien stood in the doorway for a while, his faded blue eyes scanning the room. There were several games of chance in progress, from five-card stud to faro and blackjack, and in places the line of men up at the bar was three deep, but nowhere could he see the face he was looking for. But he wasn't unduly concerned; it was only a quarter after seven — the night was still young.

He headed for the bar, a tall, slim

man in his early thirties, dressed cowhand fashion in creased denims, calico work shirt and low-heeled cowman's boots. The gunbelt strapped around his narrow waist held a .38 caliber Colt Lightning and his right hand rarely strayed far from its polished walnut butt.

A balding bartender raised his eyebrows when O'Brien bellied up to the bar. 'What'll it be?' he asked.

'A bottle of Forty-Rod and two glasses,' O'Brien replied.

The face that stared back at him from the back bar mirror was tanned and unlined, with a small, sharp nose set above a full, gentle mouth and between eyes that were robin's-egg blue. He paid for the whiskey and took it and the glasses to a corner table.

As he opened the bottle, he reflected that there weren't many people he'd ride seventy-odd miles to see, but when the chance had come to renew his acquaintance with Major John Gleason, he hadn't even considered passing it up.

He and John went back a long way. They'd first met eight years earlier, when O'Brien had been a Pinkerton detective and John a captain in the cavalry. They'd been thrown together with orders to track down a bunch of Comancheros who'd been selling guns to the Indians, and the long and bloody trail they'd ridden during that time had served only to strengthen their friendship. They rarely saw each other these days, but the friendship was still there.

O'Brien took a drink, his face clouding. This wasn't just a routine get-together with an old friend, though: there was more to it than that. According to John's letter, which had reached him at the Tombstone boarding house from which he operated, their meeting would serve a dual purpose.

O'Brien took out his Durham sack and rolled a cigarette. As he struck a lucifer, he ran through John's exact words for what seemed like the hundredth time. *I think you will find I have a proposition that might interest you. I can't say too much in this letter, but will explain it all when I see you.*

Unbidden, he again he found himself thinking about those gunrunning Comancheros. A shipment of Winchester '66s and the .44/.28 rimfire ammunition to go with them had been stolen from the Army, and reports had come in that they were being sold to renegade bands of Apache and Comanche.

O'Brien blew out a cloud of smoke, remembering the victims of the lightning raids that had followed; settlers who'd come west to find a new life. Some had been lucky and died in the first minutes of the Indians' attack, but others had lingered, long after the Indians had gone . . .

He remembered the despair in Gleason's eyes after they had ridden up to the scene of one especially vicious slaughter a couple of days later. It had been a kind of despair for humanity, a despair O'Brien understood and shared and had tried never to experience ever again. 'Christ, Carter . . . ' Gleason had asked hoarsely, 'what kind of animals could do *this?*'

It was a question for which O'Brien had no answer.

But they'd caught up with the gunrunners eventually. A well-planned attack with a troop of nine hardened veterans and the rattler's nest had been cleaned out. All except for their leader, Rocco, that was. And that had always irked O'Brien . . .

'Look lively, mister!'

O'Brien blinked, then came to his feet, grinning. 'I must be getting old, letting you creep up on me like that.'

Gleason hadn't changed a bit, he saw. He was tall, square-jawed and ruggedly handsome. His green eyes twinkled as if at some secret joke just as they always had, his complexion was still as healthy as ever and his mouth, beneath a bristling, cavalry-style moustache, was still as eager to laugh as O'Brien remembered it. And he was as immaculate as ever, too, with an open-necked woolen shirt, scarf, whipcord pants and highly polished boots.

No uniform, then.

The two men shook hands. 'Carter,' Gleason said, half to himself. 'It's good to see you. When did you arrive?'

'Just got in.'

'Tell me, still living out of a saddlebag and toting that damn Winchester?'

'What do you think?'

'I *think*, at this late date, it's about the only life you know.'

They sat down and O'Brien poured whiskey into both glasses. Gleason lifted his glass for a toast. When the whiskey had settled in his belly, he said, 'Christ, but it's good to see you again. You're looking well.'

'And you.'

From the far side of the saloon someone started to knock out an old vaudeville song on a badly tuned piano. The background chatter was warm and relaxing, and the two men talked over old times for a while, until Gleason got up to buy another bottle of whiskey.

When he came back he asked O'Brien what he'd been doing with himself over the years. O'Brien said there wasn't a great deal to tell. Since leaving the Pinkerton Agency, he'd tried his hand at just about everything. He'd been a cowboy, a town marshal, a prizefighter and a bounty hunter. These days he was a soldier of fortune, hiring himself out only when the job — and the money — was right.

'How about you?' O'Brien asked.

Gleason shrugged. 'I left the Army,' he said.

O'Brien raised one eyebrow. Gleason had always been career military — it was practically the only life he knew. 'Any special reason?'

'I guess I'd been in it too damn long, seen too much, finally got tired of living by the book.'

'So what are you doing right now? What do you *plan* to do?'

Abruptly Gleason sat forward, and O'Brien saw in his eyes a weird, moving light. 'If the cards fall my way,' Gleason said softly, 'I may not have to worry about the future. I'll be set up for life.'

O'Brien rolled another cigarette. 'This wouldn't have anything to do with the, ah, *proposition* you mentioned in your letter, would it?'

Gleason chuckled. 'Yes, it would. But I can't explain anything here — it's too public. Let's have a few more drinks, then go back to my hotel room and talk shop for a while, okay?'

Sometime later they left the saloon and walked back to Gleason's hotel in silence. The night was cold and the streets were almost empty. As they walked, O'Brien tried to judge how much his friend had changed over the years. On the surface he seemed as authoritative and confident as ever. But there was something else, too, a kind of uneasiness that all the laughter and idle chatter couldn't disguise. His eyes moved constantly, suspiciously, as if he were afraid of something. But O'Brien kept his mouth shut, figuring that he'd learn everything in good time.

When they entered Gleason's room, Gleason locked the door behind them. 'Carter,' he said uncomfortably, 'let's just get one thing out of the way first. What I'm going to tell you now mustn't go any further. And before you start thinking I don't trust you, I *do*. But when I tell you this is big, I mean it.' He paused, watching O'Brien warily. Then: 'What do you know about the Lost Life?'

O'Brien frowned. 'It's a mine, isn't it? Down in Mexico somewhere.'

'Baja California, to be precise,' Gleason said. He pulled two chairs up to the bed and signed for O'Brien to take one. Next, he took a valise from beneath the bed, unlocked it and took out a map, which he unfolded and set down on the sheets. 'About six months ago I was down in Mexico, letting off a little steam after leaving the service. That's how I came to find out all about the Lost Life and the fortune in silver it holds.'

Briefly he recounted the legend of the hidden mine.

In 1832, an old farmer named

Estaban Morito, sensing the end of his life to be near, had gone up into the Sierra de San Pedro Martir to die. For some time he had wandered in the wilderness, until he happened upon a box canyon whose walls were veined with pure silver.

Galvanized by his unbelievable good fortune, he was able to dig a chunk of silver from the canyon wall and start back for his home town of Agua Blanca. He was careful to make a rough map of his route, to be sure he could find his way back to the canyon. He drew the map on a square of old cloth, using his own blood for ink.

When he returned to Agua Blanca, he enlisted the help of his only friend, a *peon* named Pedro Margulies. It was agreed that they would go into partnership together, using the money they would make from the sale of Morito's chunk of silver to finance them. Morito left the silver and the map with Margulies, but that very same night Morito's heart gave out, as he had known all along that it would, and he died.

'Margulies didn't do anything about the canyon,' Gleason continued. 'He was a poor, uneducated man married to a bottle of tequila. He believed there might be a curse on the silver canyon, a curse that had already claimed his friend Morito, and he had no desire to become its second victim. So he buried the chunk of silver and the map, and as the years passed, he forgot all about them.

'But then one night he got drunk in a little cantina in Mexicali and started shooting his mouth off about the canyon. That's what started the whole legend off. Until then, about twelve years ago, nobody even suspected there could be a hidden lode up there.

'Now, men know the canyon is located somewhere along here,' he said, running an index finger from north to south along the map where Baja California was shown, and in particular the Sierra which ran along it. 'But to this day it remains hidden. Given the nature of the terrain, it may never be discovered, unless whoever goes up there has Morito's map.'

Gleason sat back, as if expecting O'Brien to speak, but O'Brien said nothing. Gleason continued, 'Pedro Margulies disappeared shortly after he'd boasted about the canyon. He was never seen or heard of again. According to the story, he had the silver and the map. That meant he was the only real link with the canyon. Without him, anybody going up to the Sierra might just as well look for a needle in a haystack.

'Well, it turns out Margulies died about eight months ago. But before he went, he passed the map and the chunk of silver on to the friend who'd looked after him in the last months of his life. This friend, feller named Pablo Ruiz, put the word out that the map and silver were for sale. I heard about it, got my team together and struck a deal with him.'

O'Brien spoke at last.

'Team?'

'I knew I couldn't handle this thing all by myself,' Gleason replied. 'But after so many years in uniform, I realized I didn't really have any friends on the outside, so I had to do the best I could. I drafted in a couple fellers I met in the Army, who'd mustered out about the same time as me. They're good men, Carter. One's a sergeant, a good, dependable man name of Dave Morton. The other's a private, a kid in his twenties, still a little wet behind the ears but a fast learner, and honest as the day is long. That's Frank Drew.' Gleason gave a brief tic of a smile. 'When this came up, they were glad to throw in with me.'

'I'll just bet they were. Where are they now?'

Gleason frowned. 'That's why I'm telling you all this, Carter. You see, shortly after I struck a deal with Ruiz, he was approached by another interested party by the name of Jose Ortega. Ortega wanted the canyon for himself. Badly.'

'How badly?'

'Bad enough to try and kill us, Ruiz included, when he found out that I'd already purchased the map. We left Mexicali in a hurry and went into hiding. That's when I decided to contact you. Carter, I want you to be a partner in this venture, in return for handling the ... *security* of the expedition.'

So that was it, O'Brien thought; strong-arm man to handle the fighting while Gleason and the others dug silver out of the hidden canyon — provided, of course, they could find it in the first place.

'I'm financing the entire expedition,' Gleason went on. 'Over the years I've saved my money. So I take forty percent of whatever we find. You three take twenty percent each. Ruiz has already been paid off. He's only coming with us because he's too scared to go back to Mexicali.'

O'Brien said, 'Who exactly is this Jose Ortega?'

Gleason smiled grimly. 'A tyrant,' he answered shortly. 'He owns a large part of the country and lives just outside La Paz. He built up his empire out of the copper industry in Baja California. He works his men until they drop, understands nothing about humanity but everything about profits and how to make them. He's the kind of man who will sooner have you shot dead to get what he wants rather than try to bargain with you. He's a bastard.'

O'Brien nodded. 'Do you know the Sierra at all?'

'Not too well.'

'Then it's about time someone educated you, *amigo*. It's one hell of a country. You've got vegas, timber, creeks and waterfalls, sure, but you also get rocks, deserts and great empty patches without any water at all. You have rain up there during the summer — about now, in fact — and whole areas change. Rocks and boulders get worn or washed away, little arroyos start filling, flowers and plants just

15

spring up overnight.' He took out his Durham sack and rolled another cigarette. 'Do you really expect a forty-five year old map to be accurate today under those conditions?'

Gleason shrugged. 'That's the chance we have to take,' he said.

'It's a hell of a long one.'

'Maybe not as long as you think,' Gleason replied. 'There are two reasons why I believe the map is worth having. First, Morito probably only put landmarks on his map that were as close to permanent as you could get. That map was to lead him back to his fortune, remember, so he'd have been very careful about what he chose to draw on it. Secondly, whether the country has changed or not, I believe that map gives us a better chance of finding the canyon than anyone else.'

O'Brien wasn't completely convinced, and said so.

'Ortega is a businessman,' Gleason went on. 'Do you think he'd bother with the map if he thought it was worthless? If only half of what the legend says is true, there must be at least a million dollars worth of silver just waiting to be had. Twenty percent of that's an awful lot, Carter.'

'Why can't you just file a claim on the land to get Ortega off your back?' O'Brien asked.

'Because he's got the assay office in Mexicali, as well as most of the *federales*, in his pocket . . . and until we dig enough silver out of that canyon, we can't fight back. But once we've turned some of that silver into hard cash, then we can hire the best lawyers to file our claim and make it stick.' He paused. 'It's going to be rough, Carter, no two ways about it. No man's a friend down there until he's proved it beyond all doubt. But . . . '

But . . . O'Brien thought. As much as he hated to admit it, the job appealed to him.

'All right,' he decided. 'We'll give it a whirl.'

Gleason's face went slack with relief.

'Now, correct me if I'm wrong,' O'Brien told him, 'but the situation as I see it is this: Ortega's tried to kill you once to get his hands on the map, and judging from his reputation he'll probably try again. Now, he doesn't know where your men are hiding, but could he know you're in Tucson?'

'Maybe, but I doubt it'

'Even so, let's not take any chances. Where are your men?'

'Just outside of Agua Blanca. There's a cave behind a waterfall there. It's safe enough, nice and deserted.'

'How far is Agua Blanca?'

'A little over three hundred miles.'

'Sooner we get started back there, then, the better. We'll need supplies and a packhorse. See to it tonight, if you can. Then we'll leave Tucson tomorrow, early. We'll go quietly while the town's still asleep, got it? And every mile we ride, we keep our eyes open. From now on, we don't leave anything to chance.'

With the first gray light of false dawn streaking the sky next morning, they met at Gleason's hotel and made their way along the near-deserted street toward the livery stable. They saddled up in silence, O'Brien checked the mule's packs to make sure the weight of their newly purchased supplies had been distributed evenly, and then led his roan to the stable doorway. The sky was a watery gray. On the street there was no sign of life anywhere. He turned back to Gleason, who was leading his own magnificent palomino from its stall.

'Ready?' Gleason asked expectantly.

O'Brien nodded, going over to the waiting pack-mule. He took up the line and, still holding it, stepped into his own saddle. They clucked their mounts to an easy walk.

Soon Tucson fell behind them.

They traveled south through large areas of grit and salt, around clumps of rock and large, towering boulders, and as the hours ticked away the sun climbed higher and beat down on them with an almost fearsome heat.

It was almost three in the afternoon,

and they had come perhaps twenty miles, when the shot rang out.

The bullet left a ragged score across O'Brien's saddle horn, and even as he began to swear he was also falling and tearing his old and trusted Winchester 'One in One Thousand' from its sheath. He hit the ground hard and started to roll, came up against a sharp rock and cursed at the pain it drilled into his shoulder. Then he leapt over it to get some cover between himself and —

A second thunderous volley echoed across the plain. O'Brien glanced over the rock, saw his own horse and the pack-mule galloping away. Gleason was fighting to keep his stallion under control and even as he turned it toward the cover of some boulders fifteen yards away, bullets began to kick up dust behind its skittering hooves.

They'd been caught on a sandy trail leading through two high walls of rock. Damn! O'Brien clenched his teeth. He should've been more alert! But everything had gone so well, all day . . .

He levered a shell into the Winchester and squeezed off a shot at the high rocks seventy yards away. Its roar shattered the warm air but did little else.

They were hiding up there somewhere, whoever *they* were. But how many of them? He kept his head down as the next volley of shots whined around him, chipping rock from the boulder he had chosen for cover. He listened to the booming of long guns and the higher, shorter report of handguns. There were four or five of them up there, as far as he could judge.

To his left, Gleason had taken cover in some brush and was pumping rounds from his cavalry-issue Springfield .45/.50 into the rocks. From his position, O'Brien could see the sun reflecting from two rifle barrels on the lip of the rock wall.

He wished he knew exactly how many men were up there, but knew there was only one sure way to find out — by somehow getting up there behind them.

As the bushwhackers continued to

return fire, O'Brien sucked a breath and launched himself over the rock. He ran zigzag, bent double, the Winchester clamped tight between his fists, toward the rock wall. To further throw off the aim of the men up there who meant him nothing but ill, he threw himself behind a patch of brush, rolled, came up again and continued running. His shoulder hurt like hell and he was starting a stitch.

Bullets kicked up dust around him and he dived behind a low, oval boulder. For a moment nothing existed then but the pounding of blood in his ears and the warm air scorching his throat as he drew it in. Then he began to slide forward on his belly, walking on his elbows to the far end of the boulder. He brought his feet up under him, took one more deep breath, and launched himself out into the open again.

Their aim was getting better, he noted as the rock wall came closer. There were a couple of times when he'd have been hit if he hadn't kept darting this way and that.

But then he reached the wall and turned, putting his back to the seamed rock while he regained his breath. There was no danger of one of them leaning over to shoot him from above — Gleason would see to that.

Now he ran along the base of the rock wall until he came to a jumble of boulders. Between these was a series of dusty switchbacks leading to higher ground, and the bushwhackers. O'Brien bent double, moving forward cautiously, and always ascending. After a time he was in a position from which he could see their horses, tethered to some brush and stamping or shifting nervously, on the gentle slope about thirty feet above him. There were four of them.

He levered another shell into the Winchester, then continued to climb. He kept the rifle pointed at the trail in front of him. Obviously they'd seen his dash for the base of the rock wall and guessed what he was up to. No doubt they'd sent a man back to guard the slope.

Even as he thought it he heard the high-pitched whine of a .45 caliber slug and threw himself backwards behind some rocks at the side of the trail. Someone was up there, right enough! Hardly pausing, he threw himself straight out onto the trail again, saw by the startled look on the gunman's features that he'd done the right thing, the thing the gunman least expected him to do — come out hell-for-leather, shooting.

The roar of the Winchester seemed to dwarf the shot that came from the gunman's Peacemaker, and O'Brien's bullet pushed him backwards, hard, slamming him against the rocks and punching a messy, killing hole through his chest.

Even as the gunman dropped loosely to the ground O'Brien continued upwards, staying close to the rocks and constantly scanning the terrain ahead for any further trouble.

There was none.

When he got close to the skittish horses he flopped down onto his belly and began to slide forward. His progress now was slow but absolutely silent. At last he was able to peer around a dried out patch of scrub and study the bushwhackers.

They lay on their bellies, careful to stay low, and their heads bobbed and weaved as they constantly looked for an opening. One of them used a Winchester and the other two handguns. A mist of gun smoke hung about them on the hot, still air. The sound of gunfire and the stench of cordite was almost overpowering.

In an ideal world O'Brien would get the drop on them, separate them from their weapons and send them back from whence they'd come. But this wasn't an ideal world and never would be. Men like these, back-shooters, killers-for-hire, men unburdened by conscience, only ever played the game one way, and that was for keeps.

So it was him or them, then; and he

didn't plan on cashing in *just* yet . . .

He propped the Winchester against a nearby rock and drew the Lightning. The .38 fit his palm like the handshake of a friend.

He stepped out into the open just as one of the bushwhackers rolled onto his side and started fishing fresh rounds out of his gunbelt. 'Those bastards're more trouble than they're worth,' he said over the gunfire.

Then he saw O'Brien.

O'Brien saw his eyes, bereft of human feeling long ago. The face was dried-out, gaunt, burned by sun and wind and coated with stubble.

In the awful moment when he saw O'Brien standing there, the Lightning in his fist and aimed his way, the look on his face was almost painful to behold. A silence suddenly settled upon them, as if his two friends realized just what was behind them. Even Gleason stopped shooting.

Then:

'*Hold it!*' bawled O'Brien, knowing

they would do no such thing. '*Now!*'

'*Jesus Christ . . .*'

The bushwhackers turned and tried to make a fight of it.

Tried.

O'Brien fanned the .38, moving the barrel from left to right and back again. His bullets punched red holes into the three gunmen. The first took one in his throat and fell back, choking. The second managed to trigger a shot, but it was hasty and went wide. O'Brien put two slugs in his chest. The third man started to scrabble backwards, getting to his feet. He leveled his Winchester and O'Brien emptied his Colt, planting one shell in his chest, the other in his head.

It had taken just five seconds.

The silence came back in then, almost claustrophobic. O'Brien's ears rang with the noise of the gun blasts. He looked from one to the other of the gunmen. Even death couldn't completely wipe the cruelty from their faces.

He sagged. One part of him knew

he'd done the world a service in getting rid of them. But the other part, the greater part, felt soiled again, as it always did when the killing started.

He began to reload the Lightning. Gleason yelled his name from a long way off.

'It's over, John! Come on up!' O'Brien yelled back.

The gunman with the Winchester was still quivering, but a brief glance told O'Brien he was dead: men just didn't get up and walk away from wounds like that. The fellow with the bullet in his throat was dead, too, but the one with two bullets in his chest suddenly gave a tortured groan.

O'Brien quickly put his gun away and knelt beside him. He took the gunman's Colt and threw it out of reach, then gently turned the killer onto his back, grimacing when he saw the mess he'd made of the man's guts. He looked into the gunman's twisted face until he was sure he had his attention. Then he asked, 'Why?'

' . . . f . . . for Christ's sake, mister . . . '

'Why? And who?'

' . . . ohhh . . . '

'I can always leave you to die slow,' O'Brien said.

'You wouldn't . . . would you?'

'Let's find out, shall we?'

O'Brien began to stand and turn away.

'All right!' the gunman shrieked. 'All right . . . I'll tell you . . . but you . . . you promise . . . you'll help me?'

'Yeah.'

The word stuck in O'Brien's throat.

The killer spoke around clenched teeth while his guts spilled onto the dusty earth. 'Nathan . . . ' he said. 'Nathan hired us . . . had to . . . s . . . stop you.'

'Who is this Nathan?' O'Brien demanded.

'He . . . got spies everywhere . . . '

'Where's Nathan now? Does he work for a man named Ortega?'

But it was too late. The gunman was dead.

O'Brien turned just in time to see

Gleason coming up the slope towards him. His face was pale in the sunlight and his eyes were a little crazy as he looked at the carnage around him. O'Brien worked up some saliva and spat. Gleason stared open-mouthed at the look on his face.

'I questioned one of 'em,' O'Brien said quietly. 'They were hired by a man named Nathan. I don't know if that's his first name or his last, but the chances are he's connected with Ortega.'

'So the sonofabitch's made another attempt,' Gleason said, shaking his head. 'But how did he know we'd be here?'

Suddenly O'Brien felt very tired. 'Let's search these fellers' saddlebags. We might be able to find out more about them.'

He approached the still-skittish horses and began his search. Behind them, the smell of death began to foul the air.

2

When they finally caught up with their horses, the animals were flecked with lather, but now they were quiet and grazing on some sparse grama. The sun was sinking and O'Brien decided to make camp. He left the pack-mule with Gleason and rode on ahead to scout out a suitable site. He soon found it in a room-sized piece of flat ground protected on three sides by rocks.

As O'Brien saw to the horses, Gleason built a fire and put on some coffee. Neither of them felt like eating, but the coffee would refresh them. Sitting by the fire, but not too close that the flames would make him a good target for any unseen assassin, O'Brien cleaned his guns and thought back to the killing he'd done that day. From here on they would travel by night, he decided. Gleason could take charge of the pack-mule and leave O'Brien free to ride ahead and keep his eyes open for any sign of trouble. Ortega was bound to strike again as soon as he discovered that the ambush in the draw, had failed, but he had to find them to do so, and O'Brien wasn't about to let that happen.

His thoughts turned to Gleason's other partners, at the waterfall. Did Ortega know *their* whereabouts? Had he dispatched more killers to finish *them* off? The thought disturbed him. He and Gleason could ride all that way just to end up the victims of another ambush.

Gleason came over to the fire and sat across from him. He poured himself some coffee and sat sipping it in silence. After a while he said, 'I'll take first watch, all right?' He stood up, picked up his Springfield and checked that his Cavalry Colt was still in its covered Army-issue holster.

'John,' said O'Brien. 'How safe is this cave behind the waterfall?'

Gleason considered a moment before replying. 'Safe enough,' he said. 'There might be a couple of locals who know it's there, but I doubt they even think about it. Ruiz said it was our best bet. I trust him.'

O'Brien nodded. 'Okay. Wake me in a couple of hours.' He stretched out on his blanket, resting his head against his bullet-scarred saddle. After a while he closed his eyes, but he knew he wouldn't sleep much tonight.

They rode by night for the next two weeks, often slowly when the land offered a dozen or more suitable places for ambush. Although there was no hint of trouble, O'Brien remained cautious, his right hand never far from the butt of his Colt.

The two men had not shaved since leaving Tucson, and when they crossed the border at Veracruz they looked more like a pair of saddle-bums than would-be silver miners, which was exactly O'Brien's intention.

It was here that they purchased three stubborn but hardy little burros. They also bought three horses — a mustang and two sturdy piebalds, plus full rigs for them all — for the men waiting in the cave outside Agua Blanca. While Gleason chose the horses, O'Brien went off and bought their supplies, getting them from as many different stores as possible to avoid attracting any unwanted attention. He bought shovels, pick-axes, canned foods, flour, preserves, gunny-sacks, lanterns, bandages, carbolic and ammunition in four different calibers. As an afterthought, he also bought a couple of bottles of whiskey and some more tobacco.

Then they rode on, past Lake Tamiahua, further south into Baja — or Lower — California itself, but their progress was slower now because of the three extra horses and burros.

Baja California is a strip of land made up mostly by desolate plateaux. The *Mar Bermejo*, or Gulf of California, sepa-rates the bulk of it from Mexico proper, while the waters of the Pacific lap its western shores.

Although the land they passed through was barren and arid, O'Brien knew there was a good living to be made here, with the copper industry and the fishing and pearl diving that went on along the coast. This was by turn a beautiful land, searingly hot in summer and surprisingly cold in winter. It was also a land of silver, a vast treasure of it. All a man had to do to get it was to find it and hold it against men who wanted to take it away from him.

On the seventeenth night, Gleason drew up alongside O'Brien and said, 'The waterfall is just about a mile that way.' He pointed southeast. 'There's a little box canyon about half a mile straight ahead. We'll leave our horses there and approach on foot.'

O'Brien took the burros' lines and allowed Gleason to take the lead. His eyes stabbed the shadows for any sign of ambush, but he saw nothing except the pale and empty land. After a while they came to a small canyon, almost invisible from the trail, and they ground-hitched their animals. When they had off-saddled, they watered and grained them, then hid their provisions behind a jumble of rocks in the canyon's furthest corner.

Then they were moving again, Gleason still in the lead.

O'Brien never allowed himself to look straight ahead, but instead scanned the land around them. They moved soundlessly, and five minutes later heard the liquid sound of water falling into a pool. A moment after that they saw it through the shadows, the moon reflected in the rippled surface of the pool, the waterfall spilling more water into it like molten silver in the moonlight.

'Once you get behind that wall of water you're completely insulated from most outside sounds,' Gleason whispered. 'So we haven't got a pre-arranged signal. However, someone is on guard at all times.'

'What does that mean?' O'Brien asked suspiciously.

Gleason looked awkward. 'The only thing we can do is step out into the open and approach the waterfall, so they can see that it's us.'

'You're joking, of course.'

''Fraid not, Carter.'

'What if Ortega's men are behind that wall of water? They'll cut us down.'

'There's no other way. Someone should be keeping watch at all times to make sure only we approach the cave.'

O'Brien threw another look at the waterfall. He didn't like it, it was too risky.

'I'll step out into the open,' Gleason said. 'You stay here and cover me. The minute there's any shooting I'll run for cover, all right?'

O'Brien slipped his Colt from its holster. 'All right,' he growled reluctantly.

Gleason licked his lips, then stepped out onto the grassy bank. He kept his hands away from his sides as he approached the waterfall. From his position, O'Brien watched the wall of water for any sign of movement. He was hardly breathing. Gleason stepped closer, then followed the bank around in a gentle curve until he was standing on a pile of rocks right at the waterfall's edge. Still there was no movement from the hidden cave. O'Brien's palms felt slick with sweat. Gleason disappeared behind the waterfall.

O'Brien waited. The minutes dragged by.

Come on, come on . . .

Then Gleason stepped back out from behind the waterfall and beckoned with one hand. O'Brien came out into the open, his Colt still pointed before him, ready for any treachery. He crossed the ground quickly, a shadow among shadows, until he was at Gleason's side.

Through the darkness he saw the white flash of Gleason's teeth, displayed in a grin. Then Gleason turned and disappeared behind the waterfall. O'Brien followed.

He found himself in a tunnel that went around in a shallow curve, and at the farthest end two men were seated around a small, smokeless fire. The third was standing right next to O'Brien, a rifle held in his knobby fists. He studied O'Brien with brazen interest.

'Sergeant,' Gleason said, 'how have you been? Had any trouble?'

'Nothing,' the sergeant — Dave Morton — replied, 'yet.'

He and Gleason walked along the damp, puddled cave floor toward the fire, and O'Brien, momentarily forgotten, followed them.

In the light from the dancing flames, he saw that Morton was about forty, big-bellied and craggy. But there was nothing except power in his frame, which matched O'Brien's in height. His tattooed arms, beneath the rolled-up sleeves of his ex-cavalry blue woolen shirt, were thick and corded with muscle, and his neck was thick with well-developed ridges. His nose, with its tiny broken blood vessels, suggested that he was a drinker, but he was sober enough now and when he moved he displayed surprising grace.

Gleason shook hands with the other trooper. It was difficult for O'Brien to think of the two men as being anything but soldiers, because they still wore most of their old uniforms. This was Frank Drew. He was, as Gleason had said, in his twenties, sharp, intelligent but also worryingly naive. He grinned and said, 'Good to see you again, sir.' Gleason clapped him on the shoulder.

'Howdy, Ruiz.'

The Mexican stayed huddled over the fire. He was over fifty. His complexion was dark and he sweated a lot. His white teeth were a stark contrast to his dark face. Dressed in off-white pants and shirt with a woolen waistcoat over the top, he carried an old Navy Colt in a wide green sash, and was nervous as hell. It was obvious he didn't want to come on this trip, but with Ortega's men waiting for him back in Mexicali he had no choice.

'*Buenas tardes*,' he said softly. '*Que tal?*'

Gleason nodded, then turned. 'This is my friend, Carter O'Brien.'

O'Brien felt their eyes on him. Wiping his right palm on the back of his pants, young Drew came forward and stuck out his hand. 'Mr. O'Brien.'

'Howdy.'

Ruiz nodded and smiled, just a little. '*Buenas tardes, senor. Como esta listed?*'

Before O'Brien could reply, Morton growled. 'Talk American, greaser.'

Ruiz flinched when Morton took a step toward him, confirming O'Brien's first impression — that here, in Morton, was a man of belligerent and challenging nature: a man who liked to intimidate others because it made him feel that he was the biggest and the baddest of them all.

O'Brien said softly, '*Sta bueno.*'

Abruptly Morton turned to stare at him. 'I said speak American, dammit! A language we all understand!'

'Dave . . . ' Gleason began.

'Well, hell, I'm sick to the stomach of his yammer,' Morton snapped, and it was clear that he had abandoned any deference he had once shown his commanding officer. As far as he was concerned, they were equals now;

maybe Morton even thought he was a little better than that. 'We ought to speak the same language. That makes sense, don't it?'

'Sure, Dave. That's what we'll do from now on.'

Morton stared at O'Brien again, but he was speaking to Gleason when he said, 'This is him, huh? The trouble-shooter you said you could get for us?' Now his eyes focused on O'Brien. 'You really all you're cracked up to be? You don't look so hot to me.'

'He killed four men on the way down here,' Gleason said.

Morton spat into the fire. 'Oh yeah? Which way were they facing when you shot 'em?'

'All right, Dave, that's enough!'

Morton's dark eyes held O'Brien's for a long moment. Tension hung heavy in the warm air. Gleason stepped between them. 'Come on, now. What's got into you, Dave?' When Morton didn't reply, Gleason said, 'Look, let's forget it, all right?'

Morton turned on his heel and went to sit by the fire.

'Hell, he's only sore 'cause he ain't had a drink in three weeks,' Drew said with a forced laugh.

'Well, there's a couple of bottles in with our supplies. You'll get a drop tomorrow, Dave,' Gleason replied. He looked at O'Brien. 'Let's talk.'

They sat around the fire while Drew poured coffee into enamel mugs and passed them around. Then Gleason said, 'You got the map there, sergeant? And let's have your report while we're at it.'

Morton passed across a scrap of yellowed material spattered with brown marks. He handled it almost reverently, and when he took it, Gleason did likewise. As he unfolded it, Morton said, 'We've seen nothing unusual for the past week, but the ten days before that a lot of Ortega's men rode through, likely searchin' for us.' He paused, then asked, 'D'you think he's given up on us?'

'No,' Gleason replied. 'We were bushwhacked by some of his hired killers on the way down here. They're the four men I was telling you about. O'Brien settled their hash.'

'They knew you were going to Tucson, sir?' asked young Drew.

'Apparently.'

Morton remained silent and Drew started chewing at his bottom lip. Gleason laid the old map out on the rocky floor and for a moment everyone just stared at it. It was crudely drawn, and showed a series of landmarks, but gave no scale or direction. There was what looked like a meadow, a couple of stands of timber, a creek, some boulders, four large crosses and a box with part of the fourth side missing: the canyon of silver.

'Have you got the latest map there, Dave?'

Morton passed a second map across to Gleason, who unfolded it and laid it next to Morito's original. 'Now, from the look of it,' Gleason said almost to himself, 'this meadow here would link up with the one on this map. See how they're both roughly the same shape?'

From around the fire there came grunts of assent.

'That means these four crosses must be . . . Agua Blanca . . . Santa Catarina . . . Lazaro Cardenas and . . . Santa Clara. Do you all agree?'

'Sir,' said Drew. He spoke for them all.

'Now, by making a third map,' Gleason went on, 'using Morito's original and this store-bought copy, we can figure out the distance, direction and trail we should take.'

Automatically Morton passed Gleason a pad and pencil. The major began to draw.

'What makes you so special, then, O'Brien?' the sergeant asked suddenly.

'How's that again?'

Morton shrugged. 'You don't look so tough to me, that's all. The major told us you were an all-round fighting man, just the kind of feller we needed to watch our backs on the way up into that Sierra.' He gave a short, harsh laugh. 'You look kind of harmless to me.'

Ruiz and Drew were watching them both carefully. Gleason looked up from his map-making, started to speak, but was drowned out by O'Brien.

'Tell you what,' O'Brien said softly. 'Let's step outside for a moment.'

Morton blinked at him. 'Huh?'

'I want to show you something. Some qualifications I have.'

'Carter — '

Not once did O'Brien take his eyes off Morton. 'No, John. I want Morton here to know right from the start what kind of man you've brought in.'

'Right!' Morton snapped before Gleason could object. He stood up quickly, moved around the fire, a fierce grin splitting his battered face. This was exactly what he'd been after: a good fight. He thought he'd go crazy stuck in this cave with just Drew and the greaser for company, but now the prospect of beating up the out-sider sent the blood pulsing through his body in expectation. It had always been that way with him.

O'Brien stood up as Morton started

for the cave exit. As he went past, O'Brien tapped him on the shoulder and said, 'Hold on a minute.'

Morton turned.

O'Brien's hard right fist struck him square on the jaw, pushing him back three steps. Morton fell heavily, made a little moaning sound, then rolled onto his side, limp.

'Jesus!' Drew whispered.

Ruiz crossed himself and Gleason made a sound of anger. O'Brien shook his wrist to get a little feeling back into it. He ignored the waves of pain running the length of his arm, put there by the force of the blow, and sat down again. Considering Morton was about fifty or sixty pounds heavier than he was, O'Brien was reasonably pleased with the punch.

Gleason said, 'Carter, let's just try and keep the peace, huh?'

'He was spoiling for a fight and you know it.'

'But — '

'No buts, John. You just draw your map, all right?'

Gleason bit off his reply.

Of course Morton had been spoiling for a fight, and O'Brien had put a quick finish to it. But he would have to pay for it somewhere along the line. Knowing Morton as he did, he knew the sergeant wouldn't let it go at that. He wasn't worried for O'Brien — Christ, O'Brien could take care of himself. It was just that their task was formidable enough as it was, without personal confrontations making things worse.

It took him half an hour to draw a reasonably accurate map which merged the crudely formed illustrations of Esteban Morito with the more clearly defined features of the store-bought map, and when he finished he said tiredly, 'We should get to the foothills of the Sierra without too much trouble. It's a more or less straight run southwest for twenty miles. After that, it's just a question of following the trail — and keeping our eyes open.'

'Right,' O'Brien agreed, studying the map. 'Here's how we're going to do it.

First light, I'll go check on the horses and burros. When I come back, we all have a nice long sleep.'

'Why?' Drew asked.

'From now on, we travel at night,' O'Brien explained. 'At least until we're well into the hills.'

'You think Ortega's men are still out there?'

'Someplace, yes.' O'Brien picked up the enamel cup and finished his coffee. 'We move out at two-thirty, morning after next. That gives us about another full day here. All right?'

'All right, Carter,' returned Gleason. 'Anything you say.'

Morton came to while O'Brien was out seeing to the horses. He sat up, shook his head and looked slowly and carefully around the cave. Drew was at the entrance, sitting with his rifle across his lap. Gleason was asleep by the fire. Ruiz was playing idly with a piece of string.

'Where's O'Brien?' the former sergeant asked thickly. Standing up with a grunt of pain, he staggered toward the wall of water and thrust his head into it.

'He'll be back soon, Dave,' Drew replied quietly. The pale sunshine of early morning illuminated his almost pretty features and showed up the lines of worry that were etched into them.

Morton staggered away from the waterfall, feeling his jaw. Mumbling oaths, he opened and closed his mouth a few times, then felt his teeth. Satisfied nothing was broken, chipped or otherwise loosened, he turned to Ruiz. 'Get me some coffee, greaser.'

'*Si, senor*,' the Mexican replied, knowing better than to refuse.

'And talk American,' Morton growled. 'Where's O'Brien gone, anyway?'

Drew took his eyes away from the tranquility of the plains beyond the waterfall. 'Gone to check the horses and supplies.' He seemed about to say more, but at that moment he caught a faint noise from beyond the wall of water. 'That's O'Brien,' he said, then looked at Morton. 'Just take it easy, will you, Dave?'

O'Brien slipped into the cave. He

threw a brief glance at Morton, then said to Drew, 'Gleason still asleep?'

'Yeah.'

'Wake him up.'

Morton stepped forward, his big fists bunched. He looked eager to use them, and as Drew headed for the back of the cave, he said, 'Me and you got some unfinished business, O'Brien.'

'Lay off me, Morton. This is more important.'

O'Brien pushed past him, heading for the back of the cave, where Gleason was getting to his feet, his face puffed by sleep. 'What is it?' he asked, frowning. 'Not the animals or the gear?'

'No,' O'Brien said, taking the coffee Ruiz had poured for Morton and downing it in a couple of gulps. 'Another one, *por favor*.'

'What is it?' Gleason prodded.

O'Brien felt their eyes on him. He stared into Gleason's face and said, 'Rocco.'

Gleason let out a long breath. His eyes went down to the cave floor, then back up to O'Brien again. 'The same Rocco?' he asked quietly.

O'Brien nodded. Yeah, it was the same Rocco; *Nathan* Rocco, who'd led the gun-running Comancheros he and Gleason had been after eight years before.

The man was a big-bellied Mexican-American half-breed with a dark, stubble-dotted face and almost black eyes: a large, cruel-natured man who carried a Meteor shotgun and wore crossed bandoliers. He was a cold-blooded killer who preferred to use a ten-inch Union Pacific blade for his close-up killing.

Nathan Rocco, who'd escaped the raid O'Brien and Gleason had planned all those years before . . .

'Where?' Gleason asked.

'About a mile and a half from here. He's got thirty men with him.'

Gleason smiled bitterly. 'So *he* was the Nathan that bushwhacker was talking about back at the draw. Nathan goddam *Rocco*.'

Drew asked, 'This Rocco, does he

work for Ortega?'

O'Brien nodded. 'It's likely. The way I figure it, Ortega's sent men out all over the country to find us. He must want that silver even worse than you thought. It just so happens Rocco's been given this area to search.' He took the second cup of coffee with a nod of thanks.

'We'd better move out right away,' Gleason said.

O'Brien agreed. 'They might not find *us*, but they'd be sure to come across the horses and supplies. So here's the way we'll do it. We'll go to the box canyon and get everything ready so that we can move out at a moment's notice. If there *is* any trouble, everyone moves out fast. Leave the fighting to me and Morton.'

'What was that?' Morton frowned.

'You heard,' O'Brien told him gruffly. 'Now, if possible, we'll stick to our original plan and move out under cover of night. But if Rocco and his men look like getting too close, we'll make a run

for it. All right? Right, let's get everything together. *Move!'*

'Just who is this Rocco then, Gleason?'
Morton asked.

Gleason gave him a grim look. 'A
ghost,' he said. 'From our past.'

While the others gathered everything
together and Ruiz kicked damp earth
over the fire, O'Brien rolled himself a
cigarette. 'How's that for coincidence?'
he asked softly, 'Rocco being here, after
all this time.'

'Working for Ortega, too,' Gleason
agreed. 'Carter, I hope it doesn't come
to a fight, but if it does . . . well, you
know what it means.'

'Yeah,' O'Brien replied. 'It means we
get the chance to finish that gun-
running case once and for all. After
eight God-damn years.'

3

The sky was growing heavy with storm clouds as O'Brien led them away from the hidden cave, running silently and in single file into the surrounding brush. They reached the box canyon without incident, then busied themselves getting their equipment packed and ready for any sudden departure.

'Whiskey,' Morton said when he saw the two bottles O'Brien had brought along. Despite the gravity of their situation, the former sergeant didn't seem especially worried. He allowed himself a grin as he uncorked one of the bottles and took a long pull.

'Go easy on that,' O'Brien warned him.

Morton capped the bottle and packed it into a gunnysack, then stamped across to where O'Brien was standing. 'You think you're it, don't you, just 'cause Gleason brought you in from outside. Well let me tell you something — you keep out of my way or else I might just have to whip you into line.'

'Like you did last night, you mean?' O'Brien asked mildly.

'Why — '

O'Brien made no move to defend himself against Morton's upraised fist. Instead, he stared into the sergeant's eyes and said, 'Don't think you scare me, Morton. It'll be a pleasure to have it out with you once and for all. But *after* we get through this.' Pointedly he added, 'And not before.'

'I hope that's a promise, O'Brien.'

'One you can bank on,' O'Brien replied, then turned and went over to Drew, who stood at the entrance to the canyon, Springfield clasped tightly in his hairless hands as he kept watch.

O'Brien stared out over the flat land before them. There was no sign of Rocco or his men, but it was still only mid-morning and if, as he suspected, they were searching systematically for Gleason's party, they could show up here at any time. Maybe they would find the canyon, maybe not. But if they did . . .

'Keep your eyes peeled, Frank,' O'Brien said softly. 'You sight anything I ought to know about, you come and fetch me.'

Overhead, the sky darkened dramatically. They were in for one of those summer storms O'Brien had told Gleason about back in Tucson. That could work for or against them. O'Brien felt his belly tighten. As much as he wanted to get even with Rocco, he didn't want to fight, not just yet. If they could move out under cover of darkness without being seen, so much the better. Rocco could wait until O'Brien was ready to deal with him.

'Looks like rain,' Gleason remarked bleakly.

O'Brien agreed. 'We'll move out when the storm breaks,' he said. 'It'll be hard going, but the storm'll cover our tracks, and that's about the only thing that's going to stop Rocco and his men from following us.' He watched Morton flexing his arms and walking around in a tight circle. 'You explain that to the others. I'm sick of Morton jumping down my throat all the time.'

'I just don't know what's gotten into Dave,' Gleason admitted. 'He was always a bit too big for his boots, but — '

'He didn't like the idea of you bringing me in, is all.'

'Maybe. He was my right-hand man before all this.'

'Yeah, well . . . you just give it to 'em straight, tell us where we're headed, and maybe we'll all stand a chance when the time comes.'

O'Brien relieved Drew and, as he kept watch, he heard Gleason telling the others what the plan was. As soon as the storm broke, they would move out. Gleason would take the lead and O'Brien and Morton would bring up the rear in case there was any fighting to be done. Morton started to object, but Gleason would brook no argument. They would be heading southwest: if they could clear the area without being spotted or having to fight, they could be at the foot of the Sierra within six or seven hours.

O'Brien studied the clouds overhead, turning a darker gray now as they continued to gather. Still there was no sign of anyone on the landscape before him, but O'Brien knew that didn't mean a thing. Sometimes it was all too possible to creep up on a man without letting him know you were there until you put a knife or a bullet in his back.

It took two hours for the storm to break.

Ruiz had been talking to the horses and burros, Drew checking their gear over and over again. Gleason was studying the map and Morton was complaining about the hanging around. And then it came.

First there was a muffled roar from high above, and they all looked up. The clouds were swollen and blue-black. It was a little past mid-day, but all around them the light was gray, watery and faint. *It's now or never*, O'Brien told himself. With the downpour to give them cover and wash out their tracks, conditions were perfect.

A blue-white streak of lightning split the air, struck earth and was gone. Then came another roar of thunder, two more flashes of lightning. And then . . .

All at once there was no air, no sound, nothing. The faint breeze died. The clouds hung oppressively overhead. The animals began to stamp and whinny with fear.

Then . . .

The rain came slowly, feeling its way across the country, sucked in by the thirsty land. Moments later it became a downpour, hitting them with a million needles, plastering their clothes to their chilled skin, making them squint and shiver and gasp.

'*Now!*' O'Brien yelled above another roar of thunder.

They mounted up, calming the animals as best they could, and, together with the packhorse and the three laden burros, began to file out of the canyon.

The rain was relentless. High above, thunder roared its threats. Forked lightning split the air and lit up the sky for fractions of a second before plunging them back into that eerie blackness again. They tried to keep heading southwest, but it wasn't easy: they could only rely on Gleason to lead them in the right direction, and had to keep him in sight all the time, which was almost impossible in the driving storm.

Sand, heavy with rain, dragged at their horses' hooves. Their tracks became puddles. O'Brien knew that when the storm was over there would be nothing to mark their passage. Rocco and his gun hawks would never know they'd been so close.

They were on a vast plain now, as a brief flash of lightning revealed. It was littered with boulders of all shapes and sizes. O'Brien didn't like to be out in the open, but there was no help for it.

'*O'Brien!*'

O'Brien turned. Morton was bawling at him, twisted in his saddle, his eyes half shut against the storm. Seeing that he'd attracted O'Brien's attention, he pointed off to their right and waited. O'Brien took a look.

'*Damn!*'

About a hundred yards away, eight riders, heavily clad in slickers, rode spread out in a line. They were just silhouettes in the twilight. From the casual way in which they rode, O'Brien guessed they hadn't spotted him and his companions yet.

Yet.

Were they Rocco's men? Probably. But what should he do about it?

As he turned back to Morton, he saw that the others had bunched up around him and were waiting for him to speak. Yelling above the storm, he said, 'Morton, me and you'll get under cover. The rest of you, keep moving!'

Gleason, Drew and Ruiz started moving southwest again, the packhorse and the burros trailing behind them.

'What've you got in mind?' Morton asked.

O'Brien pointed to an outcrop of boulders. 'We'll take cover in those rocks over there,' he said, 'but we won't fight unless we have to.'

'You're the boss,' Morton muttered sarcastically.

O'Brien urged the roan into an awkward gallop across the slippery ground just as another flash of lightning threw long shadows off to his left, then vanished. Thunder sounded like cannon throwing death across a battlefield. Through jarred vision he saw Gleason and the others hitting a fair pace and heard Morton's piebald coming up close behind. Turning his head he saw the eight shadowy riders, still fanned out and apparently unaware of their presence.

Then he hauled back on the reins and the roan came skidding to a halt. He threw himself out of the saddle just as Morton reined in beside him. O'Brien tied the roan's reins around a small but weighty rock, pulled the Winchester from its saddle-sheath and moved through the boulders in search of the best vantage point.

Morton hauled himself up after O'Brien, grunting as he eased himself between two large rocks. As he steadied his Springfield, he cast a cold grin at O'Brien's profile. O'Brien concentrated on the approaching riders.

They were about sixty yards away now, still spread out in a line. O'Brien guessed they'd been scouting for sign of Gleason and his team and been caught out by the storm. Instead of using their eyes, they were concentrating on getting back to camp and out of the rain.

When they were fifty yards away, O'Brien tossed a look over his shoulder. Gleason and the others were just small black dots on the plain now, almost into a group of foothills.

Then a shot boomed out and O'Brien twisted just as one of the riders fell from his saddle. The others froze, startled, trying to control their frightened mounts.

Morton gave a harsh laugh and drew a bead on another of them.

'You stupid . . . '

'They were getting too close,' Morton said, then turned back to the seven horsemen thrown into panic and triggered another shot.

O'Brien thought, *Trust me to get stuck with a goddam maniac.*

But there was no avoiding a fight now. He and Morton were stuck with the situation. These men had to be stopped from reporting back to Rocco before Gleason and the others had gained a sizeable lead. He lined the Winchester up on a rider who was pulling a carbine from its scabbard. His shot hit the man in the chest and knocked him back off his horse.

O'Brien had never had the stomach for dry-gulching, but at least now the riders were fighting back, which was something. They were using rifles and handguns. He could see the muzzle-flashes and hear the deceptively soft sound of gun-fire beneath the raging storm.

A heavy slug from Morton's Springfield had driven one man into the mud, and he was desperately trying to regain his feet. O'Brien lined his Winchester up on the man, took up the first pressure on the trigger, then suddenly said, 'No!'

Turning to Morton, he snapped, 'Do whatever it takes to get them out of those saddles, short of killing 'em!'

'*What?*'

'Once we separate them from their horses the horses'll run for home! They're already spooked by the storm!'

'Better to shoot 'em dead,' Morton bawled in reply, and, as if to prove it, aimed and fired another round.

'No!' O'Brien yelled again. 'I won't kill any man in cold blood, and while you're taking my orders, neither will you!'

Morton shrugged his brawny shoulders, and O'Brien saw a weird light in his eyes, a savage kind of joy. All at once he realized that Morton was enjoying himself, and that was wrong. Dead wrong. O'Brien drew a bead, waited a second, then fired another shot. Grazed across the rump, a prime horse reared up more in surprise than pain and slam-splashed its rider into the mud. A second shot sent the animal off at a gallop.

Through the gray sheet of rain lightning flashed, illuminating the scene in sudden, startling detail. Thunder growled its angry comment as O'Brien aimed and fired, aimed and fired, and one after another horses reared or swapped ends, stung by his lead or startled by its impact in the ground directly ahead of its forehooves, and eventually unseated their riders.

'Kill the men, you softhearted bastard!' Morton shouted. 'If you don't kill 'em now, that's all the more of 'em to follow us later!'

O'Brien knew he was right. But confronting a man face to face was one thing. Shooting men from hiding went right against the grain.

The four survivors, now set a-foot,

were still returning fire, but their aim had been thrown off by panic and the shock of ambush, and they had no cover behind which to hide down there on the plain. They were finished . . . at least for the time being.

'Come on, let's ride!' O'Brien said.

Morton laughed. His face was red with excitement. 'You kiddin'?' he asked. 'This is better'n whiskey!' He fired another round and O'Brien saw one of the men stagger backward, screaming and clutching at his chest. In that moment he threw caution to the wind, grabbed the Springfield's hot barrel and yanked it from Morton's grasp.

'*We ride!*' he yelled.

He moved back down to where the horses waited nervously. Unhitching his roan, he leapt into the saddle and thrust the Winchester into its sheath. He didn't want to wait for Morton but forced himself. Morton came down heavily off the rocks, splashed through the puddles and came up into the saddle like the cavalryman he used to be. He stared at O'Brien and suddenly, the rain, the thunder, the lightning and the half-hearted shots still coming from the survivors of the ambush were forgotten. All that existed was O'Brien and Morton.

'You made a big mistake when you took my gun off me,' Morton said. 'I'll kill you for that.'

O'Brien said, 'You're welcome to try.' Then he whirled the roan and moved off at a fast, slippery gallop. Morton matched it all the way to the foothills.

They joined Gleason and the others about seven miles further south. Gleason, tight-lipped and apprehensive, sat his palomino on a narrow trail edged with massive, misshapen rocks. His Colt was in his hand, but when he saw O'Brien and Morton round a bend twenty yards away, he sagged with relief and put it away.

Behind him, Drew and Ruiz were seeing to the agitated animals, wiping lather from their flanks and doing their best to calm them. The storm had stopped about fifteen minutes earlier, and the sky was gradually brightening again. Their tracks would be obscured, but because of Morton's stupidity, Rocco would know that they had definitely passed this way.

Gleason listened with a face of stone as O'Brien told him what had happened. Morton made a brief attempt to defend himself, but Gleason chose not to pass judgment on any of it. Instead he suggested that they try to get further into the foothills before dusk.

'No,' O'Brien said flatly.

'What?' Morton demanded.

'I said no. You remember what we agreed — that we travel by night.'

Morton looked scornful.

O'Brien said, 'No doubt there are more of Ortega's hired gunmen up here already, just circling, hoping to catch sight of us. Ortega's probably had them up here for the past three or four weeks, just in case we got through the boys he planted down there.'

'He's right,' Gleason told Morton.

'So we find a place to hole up in till nightfall. And when we move out, I want you all to make sure that everything that can make any kind of noise is tied down. We'll also tie those spare gunnysacks around the horses' hooves.'

'Okay,' Gleason agreed. 'Lead on then, Carter.'

O'Brien shook his head. 'No, you lead on. But listen carefully — and this goes for all of you. Ride well clear of branches and grass. The slightest indentation in the grass, even a break in a branch or twig will point the finger to us straight away if Rocco's got an experienced tracker in his group.'

Luckily the terrain was mostly rock, and their passage left hardly any sign. The surface of the malpais was marked minutely, but only an unusually skilled tracker would ever find such marks. An ordinary man would look for the more obvious signs, such as droppings and discarded cigarette butts. But riding in the rear, O'Brien ensured that the land remained unchanged when they passed over it.

They camped in a stale-smelling cave. O'Brien took up a position on high ground and scanned the land around them as the others slept. He could see for miles in each direction. There was no sign of life anywhere. But he could see the vast, steppe-like region which led into the Sierra. They would pass across that tonight and find another place to hole up in for the rest of tomorrow.

He thought back to mid-day, remembering the look on Morton's face as he picked off those riders. He still didn't know for sure that they *were* Rocco's men, or that Rocco was working for Ortega, but it was a pretty safe bet. He watched the sun go down, bathed in its orange glow as it dribbled into the horizon. It was almost time to move. He climbed down to the camp and nodded briefly to Ruiz, who had been entrusted with the guard duties below.

He woke Gleason, Morton and Drew, then set to work in silence, getting the animals ready for the trek ahead.

When darkness fell, they were ready to go.

It was sometime after eleven when they started up into the Sierra, and in the moonlight O'Brien could see those impassive granite peaks overlooking the San Felipe desert, even as Esteban Morito must have seen them all those years before. He shivered.

The silence was oppressive, the loneliness and desolation depressing. Occasionally, silver-lined clouds drifted across the moon, throwing everything into shadow. When this happened they stopped, waited, then moved on like ghosts once the pale night-light came back. They rode in single file, O'Brien in the lead now, Morton bringing up the rear.

The night was cold. O'Brien felt the bone-numbing chill eating right through his clothes. All around him, large boulders were spread across the vast, treeless plain, scattered like the toys of a gigantic child. The simile was uncommonly imaginative for O'Brien, and he didn't like it at all. But there was something about this place that seemed to change a man's outlook, made him believe in ghosts and ghouls and were-creatures like those said to haunt the swamps down South . . .

The higher they went, the less cold O'Brien began to feel. Deeper and deeper they went into the range, too far in to turn back now, even if they'd been of a mind to. Somewhere, far off, a gray wolf howled mournfully, and one of the horses whickered. They moved on.

O'Brien started to feel a little light-headed. It had been a hell of a day, and added to the killing and the storm they'd ridden through was the strain of the job at hand. He stifled a yawn. He regretted his lack of sleep and knew he'd been a fool not to share guard duty with the others.

They stopped once, to water their animals and enjoy the feel of cold water against their own throats. O'Brien checked the time: it was just past one in the morning. They could make another three or four miles at this walking pace, then he would ride ahead to find a place for them to camp through the coming day.

They moved off again, went for perhaps an hour without seeing anything, until —

O'Brien reined in and slid soundlessly from the saddle, motioning the others to silence and for them to dismount.

Morton growled, 'Now what's — '

'Shhhhhh!'

'What is it, Carter?' Gleason asked worriedly.

O'Brien pointed. Slightly to their right, about a hundred yards off, was the faint orange glow of a fire. Gleason let out his breath. O'Brien studied him.

'Keep everything quiet and don't move unless you have to,' he said. 'I'll be back directly.' He handed his reins to Gleason.

'Carter, what — '

'Just do what I say.' And then he was gone into the night.

He moved like a wraith, running silently, Colt in hand. He moved from one patch of shadow or cover to the next, zigzagging, sometimes going the long way around, but always heading for the campfire. The closer he got, the slower he went, taking time to check for guards and make sure there were no alarms — loose pebbles that might rattle underfoot, lengths of twine hung with empty cans.

There was nothing.

He fell to his belly, scrabbled along like a snake, rolled into a patch of scrub and came out on all fours, moving swiftly nearer. And then, hiding behind another patch of brush, he saw them.

There were five of them, all dressed cowhand fashion. But as he studied their faces, flushed with the warmth of the flames, he could see the same hard look in their eyes that the killers back at the draw had had.

Ortega's men?

Almost certainly.

One of them, wearing a battered sombrero and corduroy jacket and pants, was filling a mug with coffee. His hair was long and sandy, falling almost collar length from beneath his hat.

' . . . of the time,' he was saying. 'How long's it been now? Two weeks, right? Some of the others've been here a month.'

'Relax, Bob,' said a second man. He wore a dark Stetson and a heavy woolen shirt. 'Rocco said he'd send word if he got 'em down on the plains.'

'Christ, this coffee's cold,' a Mexican *vaquero* said.

'So make some more,' the first speaker told him harshly. 'I still think it's a waste of time.'

'We're getting paid for it, so why worry?'

'I agree with Bob,' said the fifth man, a wide, bearded fellow in denims. 'There's nothing happening up here. I betcha Rocco's caught 'em and killed 'em and just not bothered to tell us.'

'He wouldn't not bother to tell *all* of us, would he?' argued the man with the Stetson. 'Otherwise he'd get thirty sore gunnies after nailing his hide to the wall.'

'Maybe.'

'No maybe. I know Rocco. He's all right.'

The man with the sombrero grunted. 'I'm gettin' some shuteye.'

'All right, Bob. I'm turning in myself.'

'Got an early start tomorrow,' the man with the beard muttered. 'Just like every day. An early start and a day full of riding in circles, keeping watch for a bunch of — '

'Goodnight, Cole.'

The bearded man did not reply immediately. Then: 'G'night.'

O'Brien began to slide back through the shadows, considering what he had heard. They were Rocco's men, all right. From what the man in the Stetson had said, there were thirty gunslingers up here, keeping their eyes open for Gleason and his team. That meant there were twenty-five more, not counting the ones he'd just left behind, spread throughout the mountains.

Well, at least now he knew the odds.

As soon as the men they'd left alive back on the plains reached Rocco and reported the ambush, the half-breed would realize that Gleason's team had made it through their little net and were heading into the Sierra. That meant he would head right up here himself, bringing twenty or more men with him. The odds were getting worse all the time. Still, he told himself sourly as he approached the shadowy forms of the others, Morton would enjoy whittling down their numbers.

'Who . . . Carter, is that you?'

'It's me.'

As he approached them, Gleason asked, 'Well?'

Briefly he told them about the conversation he'd overheard, ending his report by suggesting they swing a wide loop around the camp. There were only five men there, sure, but if a fight broke out, the noise of it would carry in this wilderness and bring the other gunmen down on them.

'How about cold steel, O'Brien?' Morton offered eagerly. 'We go in, cut the bastards' throats and leave 'em dead in their blankets!'

O'Brien chose not to answer him, instead stepping up into his saddle. Looking down at them, he said, 'We take it nice and slow. Follow me, and don't make a noise.' His eyes, shadowy pits in the darkness, came to rest on Morton. 'If you foul up again, Morton, I'm going to take you apart.'

They moved out. It was hard work, swinging well clear of the gunmen's camp, but worth it to avoid trouble. If they could just get past this bunch, they might be able to get even deeper into the foothills and find good cover for the coming day. When Rocco arrived, he'd have no definite word on Gleason's position, and as far as O'Brien was concerned, that gave him an edge he would use to the full.

By three in the morning they were following the bend of a stream running deep from the recent rain. Along the banks, cedar trees reached skyward. Cypresses, firs, poplars and weeping willows formed a kind of avenue around them, concealing their passage. And water washed out all sign.

O'Brien spotted a rocky outcrop and dismounted, snaking along silently to scout it out. It was deserted. He climbed onto a boulder and scanned the land around him, seeing nothing. This would do, then.

They led their animals into the outcrop, Morton and Drew standing watch. After the animals had been watered and fed, and the men had eaten a little, O'Brien lay back on his saddle and sighed as the kinks in his spine ironed out. He closed his eyes, hoping for sleep but afraid that it wouldn't come.

The next thing he knew, the sun was shining on his face.

He sat up slowly. Ruiz was sitting close by a smokeless fire made of dry branches which had fallen naturally from the trees lining the stream. Seeing that O'Brien was awake, he poured coffee and passed him the cup. O'Brien nodded his thanks, looked around.

Gleason was patrolling the perimeter of their campsite. Drew and Morton were sprawled on their bellies, asleep. O'Brien checked the time. It was a little past mid-day. Another nine, ten hours and they would be off again, but this time they'd be following Morito's directions a bit closer.

He reached across and took a strip of jerky from a pile near the fire. It took some chewing but once you got it going it wasn't so bad. Ruiz was eating a pomegranate. O'Brien sipped his coffee as Ruiz, casting a look at the sleeping Morton said, '*Cuanto tiempo se necesita para llegar a la mina, senor?*'

O'Brien considered. It was a good question: how long will it take to get to the mine? He smiled at Ruiz and said,

'*Quien sabe?*' He shrugged. 'You have English, Pablo?'

Another scared look at Morton. Then: 'Yes, I have English.'

'You looked after this feller Margulies, eh? The one with the map and the silver.'

'*Si*. About the only family I ever had. An old, old man, he was, with a skin like parchment. *Si*. Pedro was a good man, a good man to me. He had his faults, but he repaid it when kindness was shown to him.'

'Like giving away the map to a fortune.'

Ruiz shrugged. 'You can't take it with you, *senor*.'

'True.'

'I just wish I could go home to Mexicali,' the Mexican sighed.

'I just bet you do, Pablo. But maybe you can ride free after we find the canyon, start a new life someplace else, where Ortega won't find you.'

'No,' Ruiz said softly. 'He has eyes everywhere. Sooner or later, he will find me. Sooner or later, he will find us all.'

O'Brien began to roll a cigarette. 'We'll see,' he said, his mind elsewhere. 'We'll see.'

4

For the next three nights they moved slowly and silently across the land, through forests of pine and oak, crossing streams, swinging wide loops around campsites and other groups of riders. They slept by day in secluded spots and listened to the howling of hungry lobos as they rode through the moonlight.

On the second night they crossed the flat Morito had drawn on his map. They were right in among those white granite peaks now, and saw bunches of racing deer and smelled the citrus fruits that grew there.

By the fourth night they had reached a stand of poplars which were also marked on Morito's map. It was here that they camped for the following day, taking turns at keeping watch and easing the knots of tension from their bodies.

During the afternoon, O'Brien sat

back against his saddle and rolled a smoke. He closed his eyes, enjoying the taste of the tobacco. It was important that the strain of night riding and the ever-present threat of sudden violence shouldn't get the better of him, otherwise, when the time came, he might not react as quickly as he should. And that could make all the difference between living and dying.

'O'Brien.'

O'Brien opened his eyes and saw Morton standing over him, his large frame blocking out what weak sunlight filtered through the trees. 'Not long now, eh?' the one-time sergeant said, smiling without humor. 'When we find the canyon, we can settle our differences.'

O'Brien blew smoke into the air. 'I thought you'd forgotten about that.'

'Not a chance, much as you'd like me to,' Morton replied. 'I'm going to beat you to a pulp and enjoy every minute of it. No more excuses then, O'Brien.' He laughed with anticipation, rubbing his big fists together.

'I suppose there's no point in me appealing to your better nature?' O'Brien asked sarcastically.

Morton shook his head, still smiling. 'I haven't got one,' he said, then turned and strode away.

That night they rode single file, but this high up, O'Brien didn't expect to find many of Ortega's men. They would all be lower down, too confident in their own abilities to consider the possibility that Gleason's group had already passed them by.

They crossed a small, winding stream, smelled grass in the air, saw vines and olives growing. Once they saw a pack of wolves running down three terrified deer. O'Brien turned away when the wolves caught up with them, but Morton continued watching with bright eyes until the action had finished.

Gleason rode up alongside O'Brien now, watching as O'Brien's restless eyes stabbed at the surrounding shadows, alert for any hint of trouble. 'We're close,' Gleason said quietly. 'According to the map, we should reach the canyon any time now.'

O'Brien threw him a glance. 'If Morito's map isn't too out-of-date,' he replied. He'd studied the damned thing more times than he cared to count. He knew it by heart, and all this time had kept a mental tally of their progress. As Gleason had just said, they should be close now. But what if things had gone wrong and they were in fact hopelessly lost?

Behind him, Morton began to whistle, and he turned sharply in the saddle. 'Keep it down, damn you!'

They rode on.

They made camp by a clump of grass and bushes, a miniature oasis amid the rocky desolation of the Sierra. As had become their custom, they ate and sat in silence. Drew and Gleason took the first watch, Ruiz and Morton the second. This left O'Brien to get some much-needed rest.

The day passed slowly, a cool day with a cloudless blue sky and small animal sounds in the air. It was all so peaceful, O'Brien thought, but he, like the others, was too keyed up to enjoy it. Tonight, if Gleason's calculations were right, they should find the hidden canyon of silver.

At last, night began to creep in behind a deep red sunset the color of blood. Time to move. O'Brien stood up and kicked dirt onto the small fire. 'Let's go.'

Gleason took the lead and the others followed in single file, O'Brien riding up and down the line of men and animals, always alert and concentrating not on the past or the future, as the others did, but on the present — and the dangers of the present.

They rode all night at a walk, as quietly as they were able. The next morning, as the sun came up, they felt hollow.

'Jesus Christ, Gleason,' Morton complained loudly. 'Where's the canyon, then? You said — '

'I know what I said,' Gleason said sharply. 'I must have been wrong. But . . . Carter, what do you say? We couldn't have been that far out, could we?'

O'Brien sat slumped in the saddle. 'I don't know,' he said tiredly. 'I really don't know.'

'It's a waste of time!' Morton snapped. He turned his horse away, jumped the animal forward abruptly, then reined in ten yards off, staring into the distance and muttering to himself.

'Major,' Drew said, walking his piebald up to Gleason. 'Don't feel too bad about it. We'll find the canyon. It's got to be here someplace. And we've made it *this* far.'

Gleason allowed himself a disappointed smile. 'You're right, Frank. It's just that . . . I was so sure we'd find it last night. Everything on the map seemed to point to it.'

O'Brien shrugged. 'Maybe we're close to it right now and we just don't know it. Study your maps again. We've got the entire day to rest up. We may find the canyon tonight.'

Gleason nodded without enthusiasm. 'Yeah, sure.'

'Major!'

They turned to Morton, who was sitting straight-backed in his saddle, pointing. Up ahead lay a vast bowl of ground, cluttered with large boulders and cypress trees. A stream, running shallow, meandered through it. And beyond that, about a hundred and fifty yards away, they could just see a narrow split between two sheer faces of rock.

The entrance to a canyon?

Gleason narrowed his eyes, almost afraid to speak. O'Brien licked his lips. *A canyon*, he thought. *The* canyon?

'John . . . ?'

'Come on,' Gleason urged, kicking his palomino into a trot.

They followed him, Morton keeping close, O'Brien edging out in front, pushing all thought from his mind except that of their security.

The sun began to climb, brightening

the land and chasing the watery grayness of early morning. The world was hushed. Nothing moved except men and animals. The whole Sierra seemed to stand in silence. Then they slowed, and, instinctively, O'Brien palmed his Colt. Gleason threw him a look of mixed emotions — hope and a kind of bitterness which threatened to swamp him if this were *not* the place.

'I'd better go first,' O'Brien said.

Gleason looked weary, but his eyes were shining. Maybe they were shining too much. 'No, Carter, I'll go in first. It's my fault you're all in this mess. I'll check it out.'

The rock walls towered above them and O'Brien sat his roan quietly while Morton and Drew swayed in their saddles, expectancy showing on their faces. Ruiz looked a little scared, no doubt recalling the legends. After all, it wasn't called the Lost Life for nothing. Gleason himself looked nervous as he walked the palomino through the narrow gap which led inside.

They waited. A breeze caressed O'Brien's face. Ragged clouds, high up, were blown slowly across the sky. And then Gleason came back through the canyon entrance. The look on his face was hard to define, but it looked a lot like disappointment.

But then, very suddenly, he grinned.

It was a wide, happy grin that threw years from him.

'Sweet Jesus!' he cried. 'We've found it! We've found the Lost Life!'

The Lost Life!

As they rode into the canyon the first thing that caught their attention were the thick black veins of unrefined silver that ran through its walls.

Then they saw the skeletal remains of five prospectors who had discovered the canyon ten years earlier and killed each other for a bigger share of the fortune it contained, and abruptly they sobered.

Gleason stepped down from his horse and walked up to one of the walls like a man in a daze. Morton and Drew laughed and clapped each other on the back. Pablo Ruiz was down on his knees, crossing himself, his dark lips moving in prayer. O'Brien slipped his gun back into its holster and slid out of the saddle just as Gleason came up to him.

He stared at O'Brien for a long time, his mouth working wordlessly, and then, suddenly, he pulled O'Brien to him and gave him a hug. 'Carter!' he said in a voice thick with emotion. 'We took a gamble and we won, dammit! We won!'

'Yeah,' O'Brien agreed. 'We won.'

But have we? he wondered. This was where the hard work really began, with the digging and the journey back across the border, fighting off Ortega's men and Rocco himself, probably. And this time it would be harder still, with a fortune in silver slowing them down. Even so, he smiled into Gleason's flushed face. He found it impossible to gauge his own reaction to the find. He was indifferent to the silver itself, but at least they had succeeded in what they had set out to do, and success was what mattered most of all to O'Brien.

'Break out the whiskey!' Morton said from behind him. 'Let's do some celebratin'!'

For once he was in agreement with the sergeant.

And so began the hard work.

O'Brien did none of the digging. He'd signed on to handle the security, and he couldn't do that with a pick in his hands. The canyon, being hidden, was unlikely to attract any unwelcome visitors, but it was best to keep watch at all hours of the day and this they did. By the end of the first day, O'Brien had worked out a rota system by which one man was always on guard and another at rest to relieve him after a six-hour stretch. The others, when they weren't resting, dug silver from the canyon's walls.

Their plan was simple. They intended to dig as much silver from the canyon as they could comfortably carry, then run the gauntlet back across the border.

The fact that their supplies were running low dictated that they stay no longer than two weeks, and O'Brien knew that at the end of it he wouldn't be sorry to head back home. Then Gleason would use some of his new wealth to hire the best lawyers to file a claim on his behalf, which should offer some protection, at least, from Ortega.

But first he and O'Brien would find a way to deal with Rocco. There was no way they could leave that score untended.

On the eighth day, Morton came up as O'Brien sat around their small fire, cleaning some sand out of his Winchester. O'Brien was a man who believed in looking after his guns, and found it restful when he worked on them. When Morton's shadow fell across him, however, he knew that the peace was about to be shattered.

Ever since their arrival at the lost mine, Morton had barely resisted the urge to pick a fight with him. Once or twice O'Brien had looked up to catch

Morton staring at him with hatred in his eyes, and he knew the sergeant's threats had not been idle. He wasn't afraid of Morton, but likewise he wasn't eager to involve himself in a fight for no good reason. Until —

'All right, O'Brien. Vacation's over.'

O'Brien looked up. 'How's that again?'

'You know what I mean. We agreed. When we reached the mine, I'd beat your skull to mush.'

'I didn't agree to that,' O'Brien said mildly.

'On your feet, mister. I've seen your sort before, in the army. Snot-nosed little know-it-alls, like the colonel back at Fort Douglas, telling me I couldn't re-enlist just because I beat up some sassy civilian who was back-talking me in a bar in town.'

'For Christ's sake, sergeant — ' Gleason said from somewhere behind them. He, like Morton, was sweating heavily and covered in dust from the canyon walls. But, unlike Gleason,

Morton was not even breathing hard from the work he'd been doing.

'Butt out, major,' Morton told him without looking around.

Gleason took a step forward. O'Brien said, 'Leave it, John.' He gave a weary sigh and got to his feet. To Morton he said, 'Let's get it over with, then.'

'Not so fast,' Morton grinned. 'You'll get yours soon enough.'

As if by mutual consent, they walked side by side a little way further down the canyon to a spot where they'd buried the skeletons of the five men who'd killed each other years before. This would be their arena.

'I owe you, O'Brien,' the non-com growled. 'For taking my Springfield away from me, for buffaloing me in the cave behind the waterfall that night . . . '

Without warning he lashed out, catching O'Brien firmly on the chin.

O'Brien was completely unprepared for the blow and stumbled backwards, tasting the warm saltiness of blood on his tongue. He heard Morton laugh and through blurred vision saw the sergeant come at him, grinning fiercely.

Then O'Brien went down on his left shoulder, rolled over and came up with a kick in Morton's guts. He felt the stale air that came out of Morton's mouth and rolled away as the non-com fell winded to his knees. Then O'Brien was up, working his mouth to ease the pain filling his jaw.

He waited until Morton got to his feet and turned on him, brows gathered in fury. A right hook, clumsily delivered: O'Brien blocked it and threw back one of his own, a tighter, more controlled jab which bloodied Morton's nose. The sergeant grunted, moved out of O'Brien's reach and danced around like a professional prizefighter. O'Brien could imagine the years of experience Morton must have had at brawling, especially in army barracks, where fist-fights were organized partly for gambling purposes, partly to settle scores and partly just for the hell of it.

Morton came in fast, hitting O'Brien

on the side with a blow meant for his belly. O'Brien half-fell away as Morton struck him on the back of the neck with bunched fists.

He elbowed the non-com hard, turned quickly, punched once with his right, once with his left, blocked a savage knee to the crotch with his thigh, and then missed with a left swing at Morton's belly.

They came apart, closed again almost immediately, each man sparring, looking for an opening. O'Brien threw a right and felt his arm jar as it landed. Morton started to fall back and grabbed O'Brien's wrist as he went down. O'Brien had to go with it or have his arm broken. He landed with a thud on his back, tried to get up but Morton, the heavier man, fell on top of him, his knees forcing O'Brien's arms down.

Morton's hairy fists closed around O'Brien's throat, choking him.

'No, sergeant!' Gleason yelled, his voice muffled by the rushing of blood through O'Brien's ears.

The pressure of Morton's fingers increased. O'Brien felt his mouth opening, his tongue licking at the air, the saliva drying on it and the blood from the cut inside his mouth trickling back down his throat. He felt his blood pounding . . .

'Mort . . . on . . . ' he croaked.

But there was something maniacal about Morton now, and it made O'Brien remember the way he'd enjoyed killing Rocco's men and how he'd relished the scene of the wolves chasing and killing the deer . . .

'No, little snot-nose!' grated the ex non-com. 'You're gonna *die!*'

Still O'Brien struggled against him, forcing the words out. 'Mort . . . on . . . riders . . . *Riders!*'

Through a misty haze, he saw Morton begin to frown. He felt the pressure leave his throat and began to suck in air. Morton pushed himself away from O'Brien, getting to his feet. 'Where?' he yelled.

O'Brien sat up, coughing. He pulled his Lightning from its holster. The sound was louder now, the pounding not of blood racing in his ears but of horses, many horses, coming nearer.

Even as they all turned, the gunmen were filing through the gap in the canyon, weapons held high, and as O'Brien and Morton got ready to defend their lives, a shot cracked out and churned up dust inches away from them.

'*Move and I'll shoot you dead!*' cried their leader.

O'Brien stared up at the man and muttered, 'Rocco.'

Gathered together and tied securely with their hands behind their backs, O'Brien and the others huddled around the dying fire, where they sat looking at the men who had invaded their canyon.

Nathan Rocco was talking to someone a few yards away. In his right hand he held his shotgun: across his broad chest were the same cartridge-heavy crossed bandoliers he had always favored.

Time seemed not to have changed him. Now in his mid-forties, he was still massive — easily six and a half feet tall — with a fat belly that strained the seams of his sweat-stained wine-red shirt. His skin was the color of milky coffee, the straggly hair sticking out beneath his sombrero raven black. He was whiskery, with glittering, soulless black eyes set beneath the buttress of a heavy brow.

Behind him, twenty dirty, sweat-smelling gunslingers had dismounted and were either seeing to their horses or studying the seams in the canyon walls with awe. One man still sat his pony, a bronzed and silent Yaqui, dressed white-man fashion. A faint breeze blew the feather in his hatband.

Rocco turned away after a moment and began to converse with the Yaqui, then he sauntered across to his prisoners, and O'Brien saw that he'd lost none of his swagger over the years. 'Well, well, well,' Rocco said, grinning. His voice was a low rasping of gravel on gravel. 'If that don't beat all. I knew Gleason was involved in all this, but I'll be damned if I knew I'd find you here as well, O'Brien.'

O'Brien only shrugged.

Gleason cleared his throat. 'You're in with Ortega, am I right?'

'I'm Ortega's right-hand man,' Rocco replied, squatting. He took out his knife and began to carve patterns idly in the sand. 'You were a fool to go for the silver, Gleason. Especially since Ortega wanted it as well. Ortega always gets what he wants, no matter what the price. And now he's got all this.' He looked around the canyon.

Gleason asked, 'What are you going to do with us?'

Rocco laughed. 'Kill you,' he said.

Gleason paused. 'How did you find us?'

Rocco put the knife away, and O'Brien felt better for that.

'We'd never have found this canyon,' Rocco replied. 'But then, you already knew that. You had the map. Without that, we stood about as much chance as anybody else — which wasn't much.

Anyway, once we realized you'd got through our search parties, we hired the Yaqui, Alvarez, over there. He used to scout for the army, then discovered he could make more money working as a free agent. After that it was easy: he could track a flea across glass. Tracking you weren't so hard. 'Course, you back-tracked a few times, went through one hell of a lot of creek-beds, but sooner or later, Alvarez always found your sign again. It took a while, but we got here in the end.'

Morton spat into the dying fire. 'Well, if you're gonna kill us, get the hell on with it, you half-breed bastard.'

Rocco smiled coldly. 'Don't try to anger me, *gringo*,' he replied, eyes alight with sardonic humor. 'It won't get you a quick death, I promise you that. In fact, I think you will all die slowly. *Very* slowly.' Again he laughed, then stood up. 'We have to get back to *Senor* Ortega and tell him the news. I will leave six or seven good men here to guard the canyon, then send some workers back so we can start mining the silver in a big way. As for you five . . . well, I'm sure we can deal with you somewhere along the way.'

He stared hard at O'Brien and Gleason, then said with sudden venom, 'You spoiled a good living for me all those years ago. Don't think I've forgotten that.'

Then he turned and left them alone.

They had to control their horses with their knees, because their arms were tied behind them and their ankles were secured together beneath their mounts' barrels. They rode in silence, because there was nothing to say, and they were surrounded by thirteen hardened killers.

The night before, they had been thrown into a corner and guarded by two men, as Rocco and the others broke out bottles of whiskey and got drunk. Their party went on into the early hours, and then they fell into a sound slumber.

But early the following morning

— today — they'd saddled up, all but seven of them, with whom Rocco had entrusted the security of the canyon. Then they left, traveling in double file back across the Sierra.

Rocco had said they were heading back to Ortega, which, if O'Brien was thinking straight, meant they were bound for La Paz. Between here and there lay only one obstacle, and, remembering Rocco's words, *we can deal with you somewhere along the way*, O'Brien went cold.

It took four days of brisk riding to reach the foothills, and as they left the Sierra behind them, O'Brien took one final look back at the towering white peaks. Now he knew better than ever why the mine was called the Lost Life. If what he suspected Rocco had in mind for them was correct, then you could add five more names to an ever-growing toll of victims.

On the fifth morning, Rocco came over to them in a particularly good mood. His grin displayed twin rows of even white teeth as he looked first at them and then at the vast plain spread out before them. Now that they had come down from the Sierra, the heat had grown oppressive again, and would grow hotter still as the day wore on.

'The San Felipe desert,' Rocco told them, lifting an arm to point. 'It stretches for a lot further than the eye can see, my friends. And it's absolutely empty. No water, no shade, no salvation.' His grin widened out. 'It's where your bones will bleach.'

O'Brien went cold in the pit of his stomach as he and the others were yanked roughly to their feet. He watched as Rocco's men gathered round, bunching their fists, barely able to hold their blood lust in check.

'I'll see you in hell, my friends!' Rocco said, smiling.

Then came the first punch, the second, third and fourth, a kick, a graze, more punches. Blood ran warm across his skin, lights exploded inside his head. Before long his whole body was shrieking with pain. To be beaten like this was bad enough, but to have your hands tied behind you and not be able to defend yourself . . .

He fell to his knees, the breath knocked out of him. In one jarred moment he saw the others taking similar punishment, and then a savage blow caught him on the side of the face and he went down, tasting sand in his mouth. Shortly after that, he blacked out and knew no more.

And then there was pain.

It caught every movement he made, even the shallow rise and fall of his chest as he breathed, and increased it, sharpened it until he thought he would scream.

He opened his eyes.

The desert looked much as it had done the last time he saw it: one vast hell of a land. The sun beat down on him as he sat up. He felt lousy. His face was puffed up and bruised, and it felt like he had a couple of busted ribs. Around him lay the battered bodies of the others, all of them still hog-tied as he was. In the silence he heard the raggedness of their breathing.

O'Brien looked around him. No horses, no water, nothing with which they might hope to survive. Rocco, the cold-hearted bastard, had left them here to die.

Drew was awake. He sat up, a few yards away, his eyes puffed shut. He was talking to himself. Ruiz, nearby, made no move, no move at all, not even to breathe.

O'Brien realized he was dead.

Gleason had taken a beating, too. When at last he woke up and tried to move, they discovered he had a broken collarbone. Morton was breathing noisily and kept losing his breath. He complained of bad chest pains. He was as pale as wax.

After that, they hardly spoke. It hurt too much to speak anyway. O'Brien checked the position of the sun. He figured they had been unconscious or semi-conscious for a day, perhaps longer. He sat with head lowered, feeling the sweat being squeezed out of him by the relentless heat.

If he remembered correctly, there was a town called San Felipe due east. That was their only chance — to walk, reach help.

At first, the others didn't want to know. Walking hurt. Walking tired them out too easy. It was easier to sit back and wait for death. Then, when O'Brien started to limp away from them, they saw his reasoning and followed him, leaving Ruiz where he had died.

Their progress was slow. On the first day they made only four miles, and as the sun sank into the hills behind them they half-fell to the earth and slept.

The following day was even worse.

By this time the sun was frying their brains and they had to keep stopping while Morton caught his breath. Drew kept talking to himself and Gleason started thinking he was back on parade duty. The sun did that to you, after a while.

Covered in dirt and sweat, sand making their eyes run, they kept walking, the effort of putting one foot in front of the other an automatic, if painful, reflex. O'Brien's lips dried up and split, his unprotected skin blistered from the terrible heat above, his tongue began to taste like a dead mouse stuck inside his sandpaper mouth. At night he shivered uncontrollably and by day he sweated out even more precious body-moisture. With no food or water, he, like the others, lost weight rapidly, lost energy, lost the will to carry on . . .

He turned and saw Gleason, Morton and Drew stumbling along in a ragged line behind him. He was almost blinded by the sun. Here they all were, weak and hungry and dying of thirst, covered from head to foot in blood, sweat, sand, blisters, cuts and bruises, with their hands tied behind their backs. And they owed it all to Rocco. That thought alone spurred him on. The others, their brains addled by the pain and heat, followed on blindly.

O'Brien fell down, and as he lay in the sand he felt the heat of the sun burning right through his torn canvas shirt, baking the sweat into his pores. He had the stink of death on him, and his hair hung in greasy strands down his face. *If I die now*, he thought, *I'll go out a mess.*

But then he got up again and kept walking, without knowing why.

On the fifth day Drew collapsed. O'Brien kicked at him. It was easier than trying to speak. Drew didn't move. He was dead.

They didn't know who they were anymore, didn't know why they stuck together, but when chill night came, it was better to huddle together than freeze alone.

And then, eight days into the desert, a sand storm blew up, fierce and biting, stinging their flesh as it whipped sand at them with terrifying force. It stung their eyes, pushed them down when they tried to stand up, stole their breath away. They lay where they fell, Morton starting to choke up blood and Gleason still yelling orders to an imaginary cavalry troop.

None of them had the energy nor the inclination to get up when the sand storm ended. It left them half-buried and unnaturally still, and in that stillness was the stillness of death.

5

When O'Brien opened his eyes he saw an angel.

She had to be an angel. With a face like that, so smooth and pale and pretty, and with Jesus Christ Himself behind her, there was nothing else she could be.

' . . . never figured on ending up . . . here,' he croaked.

He felt good. Cool white sheets caressed his body. There was no sand, no walking, no pain. He watched contentedly as she gently lifted his head and gave him a drink. Water! Cold, sparkling water, trickling down his throat. Beautiful!

'Beautiful,' he muttered. He was looking at the angel as he said it.

Then his vision sharpened.

Jesus Christ existed only in a picture on the plain adobe wall, and the angel was dressed in black and white.

A nun.

O'Brien tried to sit up, but she made a clucking noise with her mouth and pushed him back down. He was too weak to resist.

'Who . . . ?'

Her voice was light, gentle, her English good. 'Rest. You are safe now, senor. We found you half-buried in the sand two miles to the south. You have been here for five days, sleeping, often dreaming of bad things. You have shouted a lot. But now you are better. The shine in your eyes tells us so.'

O'Brien frowned. 'But . . . '

'We must pray to God and thank Him for His kindness, senor.'

She closed her eyes, clasped her hands together and started moving her lips soundlessly. A small wooden cross swung to and fro around her neck as she leaned over him. O'Brien closed his eyes for a moment, trying to collect his thoughts. He felt the bandages that bound his ribs together, and when he moved his arms, they felt stiff and numb, but better. He opened his eyes again.

'The others . . . ' he husked.

The nun opened her eyes. 'We found you and your friends two miles to the south,' she repeated.

'I know . . . but . . . '

'One of them is dead. I'm sorry, senor.'

O'Brien licked his blistered lips.

'But the other, the major, he lives.'

O'Brien relaxed on his pillow. So Morton was dead. Despite the animosity they had shown each other, O'Brien was sorry to hear it. For all his faults, Morton had been a man's man all right, full of guts and grit. But at least Gleason was still alive.

'I will send him to see you, now you are awake,' said the nun as she stood up and swished from the room.

O'Brien craned his neck, looking around him. There was a small chair, a set of drawers, a pile of clothes (his clothes, he realized, washed and repaired). Christ seemed to stare at him from the picture on the wall, and as he lay back, enjoying the softness of the mattress beneath him, he looked at it and said quietly, 'Thanks.'

Then Gleason came through the door, managing a weak smile. He looked about ten years older. The nuns had fashioned a bandage that went around his neck and right shoulder. Looking at him, O'Brien wondered what he himself must look like. Maybe it was O'Brien's imagination, or the reflection of clean sunlight off the white walls, but there seemed to be new shades of gray in his friend's hair.

'Morton,' he croaked.

Gleason sat heavily on the edge of the bed. He stared down at the floor, and as O'Brien watched, he seemed to shrink into himself. When he spoke, his voice was bitter. 'Yes. Morton. And Drew, and Ruiz.'

They were quiet for a moment, until O'Brien asked, 'Where are we?'

Gleason brightened a little. 'A poor little place called the Mission de San Tomas. It's about six miles outside San Felipe. The nuns — there are eight of them — set themselves up to do what they can for the locals, but as near as I can see, it's all they can do to look after themselves. They found us almost a week ago, brought us back here, patched us up. It was too late for Sergeant Morton, he was already dead when they reached us.'

'Yeah.' O'Brien's voice was hoarse.

'I came to some time yesterday morning, been walking around the mission ever since, trying to figure out where we go from here.'

'The . . . nuns . . . '

'They know we went into the Sierra to find the lost canyon, but I told them we couldn't find any trace of it, and that we were attacked by a bunch of robbers on our way down and left to die. They believed it.'

And then Gleason turned and punched the wall. 'Morton and Drew and Ruiz . . . all dead, because of me!'

O'Brien said nothing, waiting for the grief to pass. After a while, Gleason turned back to him and said, 'Carter

— where do we go from here?'

'La Paz,' O'Brien replied at once. 'That's where Rocco was heading, wasn't it? To report to Ortega? We'll go there, and settle with both of them, once and for all.'

'How?'

'I don't know yet. But I want Ortega, John. I've been shot at, beaten up and left to die in the desert, and I owe it all to him. Him and Rocco.'

To his surprise, Gleason snorted. 'It's a fine sentiment. But look at us, Carter. I've got a broken collar-bone and you've got three or four cracked ribs. What can we do in this condition?'

O'Brien was a lot of things, but definitely not a defeatist. 'It'll take a couple of weeks to heal,' he allowed. 'But after that we can ride.'

'For Christ's sake! Do you know how far La Paz is?'

'Couple hundred miles?'

'More like *six* hundred! And it's not exactly the best country for a couple of cripples like us to ride over, even if we could get some money to buy guns, ammunition and horseflesh!'

O'Brien closed his eyes. Gleason was right, of course. It was asking a lot to even *hope* they could get revenge, never mind justice. With La Paz six hundred miles away, and with him and Gleason still weak and waiting for their bones to mend, it would be weeks yet before they could even consider starting the journey. Even then everything depended on whether or not they could raise money to buy horses, weapons and supplies. It looked hopeless.

Bleakly, O'Brien said, 'What do you suggest, then?'

Gleason tried to shrug. 'I don't know. I really don't. But I'd sorely like to get my hands around Ortega's throat.' He was quiet for a moment, and then he studied his friend. 'If there was a way to do it . . . ' He left the sentence unfinished.

'We owe Ortega and Rocco,' O'Brien said, almost to himself. 'We owe them both, for Morton, Ruiz and Drew. I don't care how long it takes, or how I do it, but I'll tell you this much. I'm going to pay them back.'

The little white-walled mission was in a poor state of repair. When he was well enough to walk, O'Brien took a slow tour of the place and everywhere he looked he found something that needed tending. The nuns, he discovered, lived in near-poverty, but were content with their lot, so long as they could spend their limited resources on the wellbeing of the locals.

Against all the odds, there was a surprisingly fertile garden behind their small chapter-house, and one afternoon O'Brien, supported by the Mother Superior, Sister Benedict, walked slowly through the sparse grass, smelling the scents of exotic flowers and fruits that grew there. He had been up and about now for five days, had started eating solids again and was rapidly convalescing.

It was a long time before he spoke. At last, he said, 'Mother, Major Gleason and me have to be moving on soon.

We've got to get back across the border.'

Sister Benedict stopped. She was a small woman with a kind-natured face and brown eyes flecked with gold. 'America,' she said. 'It has been some time since I was there. A long time, in fact. Is it as unruly as it ever was?'

O'Brien's face was lit by a brief smile. 'Yes,' he replied. 'The thing is, we'll need horses, maybe a couple of handguns to protect us on the way home.'

She nodded. 'I cannot help you with the guns,' she said, 'but horses . . . well, there is a stable owner in San Felipe who worships with us regularly. He will allow you to take two of his horses if I write him a note. I trust you will find some way to repay him as soon as you are able?'

'Of course. Thank you.'

'We can give you a few supplies from our own stock. Not much, but a little.'

O'Brien nodded, uncomfortably aware of how Sister Benedict was studying him. 'Is there no other way you could settle your differences with Senor Ortega?'

she asked suddenly. Seeing O'Brien's surprise, she said, 'When you were unconscious, you cried out several times. Always they were the same words — Ortega, Rocco and silver. It did not take us long to make some sense of your ravings. *Senor* Ortega has done you some terrible harm. Such is his nature, for he is a tyrant. Forgive me if I am wrong, but if we could have given you guns, would you really have gone back to America, or straight to Calamajué, and *Senor* Ortega, to get revenge?'

O'Brien was unable to meet her gaze. 'All right, you've caught me out, Mother,' he said after a while. 'Yes, I admit it — it's our intention to get even with Ortega for what he's done to us, what he's taken from us, and what he did to the men who rode with us.'

Sister Benedict shook her head. 'Why must men always be so preoccupied with thoughts of revenge?'

'I don't know,' O'Brien said honestly. 'It's just the way we are.' He frowned suddenly. 'Wait a minute. Did you say

Ortega was in Calamajué?'

Sister Benedict nodded. 'Yes. Why?'

'I thought he lived in La Paz.'

'So he does. But he has property everywhere. He has for some time been eager to locate the silver canyon said to exist in the Sierra de San Pedro Martir. It is common knowledge. He moved into his *hacienda* in Calamajué recently whilst his men went into the hills in search of it.'

'And how far is Calamajué, Mother?' O'Brien asked with rising excitement.

'About ninety miles south,' the nun replied.

Ninety miles! It was a whole lot better than six hundred! For a moment O'Brien was tempted to pick Sister Benedict up and kiss her on the lips, but he stifled the urge, saying, 'I'm sorry if I've only repaid your kindness with deceit, or if I offend you in wanting to get even with a man you yourself call a tyrant, but that's just the way it is. I hope you will forgive me.'

'You must do what you feel to be

right,' the nun told him softly. 'But think long and hard before you do anything, *Senor* O'Brien, for if you make a mistake then you will have to live with it for the rest of your life.'

A week later, O'Brien and Gleason left the mission, carrying some meager provisions given to them by the Mother Superior. They walked slowly, their bodies still weak, but mile followed mile and by early afternoon they came to San Felipe. It was a large, bustling town and they entered it cautiously, in case any of Rocco's men should be there. As it turned out, they saw few Americans on the streets.

They had no money, but they could find odd jobs in order to put a stake together. They went directly to the stable-owner Sister Benedict had spoken about, and after giving him her note of introduction, were given two bony but reliable-looking cow ponies. They asked after work and were directed to a large dry-goods' supplier who was taking on strong men for loading and unloading wagons. The work was hard and the pay small, but it was a start. By the end of the first day, when they bedded down at the stable, they were exhausted.

Two weeks later, they heard of a job in San Felipe's only bank. The bank was looking for someone with education to copy important documents, and O'Brien urged Gleason to go for it. It meant more money for their grubstake and also got Gleason away from the hard manual labor of the dry-goods' supplier. Gleason went for an interview and got the job.

A week and a half later, O'Brien realized that they had managed to save seventy-two dollars. It wasn't much, but it was a lot more than they'd arrived with. He sat in on a game of five-card stud one evening at one of San Felipe's many fly-blown cantinas, and upped their stake by another thirteen dollars.

They had money and horses. The time had come to head for Calamajué.

For six days they rode hard, eating dust and sleeping rough. O'Brien still hadn't worked out a plan of action, but he'd been in this line of work for so long that he was sure something would suggest itself to him by the time they reached Calamajué.

Even so, it wasn't going to be easy. It never was. The chances were that Ortega would be well-protected, and as yet he and Gleason still didn't have any weapons.

At last they came to the town and while Gleason waited on the outskirts, O'Brien rode in and made discreet enquiries. He came back thirty minutes later with directions to the *hacienda*. They swung a wide loop around town, just in case any of Rocco's men were there who might recognize them.

By mid-afternoon they had reached a slope from which they could see the house. It was a rambling, two-storey affair with about ten rooms, surrounded by a large garden, rich with emerald green grass and dotted with bushes, flowerbeds and willow trees. Around the whole was an eight-foot high adobe wall.

Three guards patrolled the garden, with Henry repeaters tucked under their arms. If O'Brien intended going over the wall, he'd have about two minutes between one guard disappearing and the next coming around the corner.

They ground-hitched their ponies on the slope overlooking the *hacienda* and O'Brien relaxed in some shade, watching them chew on the sparse grama that patchworked the ground. His restless eyes kept coming back to the *hacienda*. The guards patrolling the grounds were as regular as clockwork.

Throughout the rest of the day people came and went on a variety of different missions. At last the sun began to set and as the sky turned deep orange, a light mist began to fall. O'Brien and Gleason ate a cold meal in silence, after which they sat quietly until full night came. Then Gleason asked, 'Okay, Carter. What's the plan?'

O'Brien smiled. Well, here it was, time to decide. 'We wait until everyone goes to bed, then I go over the wall, find Ortega and . . . '

'And?' Gleason prompted.

O'Brien let his breath out in a slow sigh. 'And I don't know,' he said. What could he do, go in and kill the bastard with his bare hands? Kill him in cold blood? 'I don't know,' he said again. 'Any ideas?'

Gleason shook his head.

O'Brien sighed again. 'Okay. I'll just have to play it by ear.'

'Christ, Carter, you've got to have a plan!' Gleason objected. 'It's going to be risky enough as it is, going in there without a gun!'

O'Brien's teeth showed white through the gloom. 'I'll get a gun from the first guard I meet,' he whispered.

He turned his attention to the *hacienda*, now glowing with the yellow light that spilled from its windows. Gleason studied his profile. He knew it would do no good to argue the point: O'Brien's mind was made up. He was going into the *hacienda* and as soon as he clapped eyes on Ortega some instinct inside him would tell him what to do. Provided he got that far.

They sat impatiently waiting for the lights at the windows to blink off. Around them, the mist, cold and damp, floated lower. Gleason sat muttering and cursing under his breath. One by one, lights began to go off. Minutes dragged into an hour, two hours. More lights went off. Three hours later the *hacienda* was in darkness, but still they forced themselves to wait. At last O'Brien checked the time: it was a little after one a.m.

He stood up. 'If I'm not back in an hour — '

Gleason rose to his feet. 'I'm going with you,' he said.

'You're more use to me here.'

'Dammit, Carter! We're in this mess because of me — '

'You're more use to me *here*,' O'Brien repeated. He looked into his friend's eyes. 'Give me an hour. If I'm not back by then — '

Gleason nodded. 'I know, I know. I

wait another hour.'

Smiling, O'Brien clapped him on the shoulder. 'I'll be back directly.'

He turned and disappeared into the shadows before Gleason had a chance to wish him good luck.

He went down the slope like a wraith, slipping only once on the slick grass. He kept to the shadows and ran zigzag, always alert. He felt naked without his gun, but there was nothing he could do about it now.

And then he was hugging the adobe wall and catching his breath, hidden beneath the shadow of a big willow which overlapped the garden. After a moment he calmed down and strained his ears for sounds beyond the wall. He heard nothing. Then he tensed.

He had picked up the faintest noise. Again! The crunch-crunch of a guard's footsteps coming nearer, on the other side. He held his breath, waiting. The footsteps came closer, closer, until they were directly opposite him. At last they died away.

When he guessed the guard must be eight or nine yards away, he sprang up, caught hold of the wall's tiled top, swung his right leg up and hooked it over. He stayed like that, hanging on the wall, until he was sure the guard was still moving away, and then he dropped into the garden. He landed quietly, any sound he made muffled by the thick grass. He scanned the shadows, saw what he wanted and picked it up.

It was a willow twig. It felt a little damp, but it would do. He snapped it.

'Huh?'

The guard's voice came back to him through the misty night air. O'Brien vanished behind the willow tree. He heard the guard turn abruptly and lever a shell into the breech of his rifle.

You've got to make this quick and quiet, O'Brien told himself.

The guard began to advance through the fog. As he got closer, O'Brien saw that he was a poncho-clad Mexican. He was poking cautiously at the shadows, mumbling.

Wait for it . . .

'Attention . . .'

And then he was close enough.

O'Brien leapt out, arms going up, hands clutching at a sturdy branch of the willow. He swung his legs out, hard, fast.

'Que — '

The guard never knew what hit him. O'Brien swung both legs out and caught him beneath the jaw. He went over backwards with a grunt. O'Brien let go of the branch, fell to earth again and almost jumped on the guard, clamping a hand over his mouth in case he was still conscious and ready to yell out.

But he wasn't. His breathing was heavy and laboured. He wouldn't be waking up for a long time yet, and even when he did, it would be some time before he felt like raising the alarm.

O'Brien took the rifle — a battered but serviceable Winchester — and unbuckled the Mexican's gunbelt. A brief glance told him the holster contained a Remington Army .44. He quickly tied it around his waist, dragged the unconscious man further into the shadows and, clutching the rifle, moved like the mist itself across the garden until he reached the cold white walls of the house. He released his pent-up breath. So far so good.

He moved along the wall, bent double, until he came to a half-open window. Cautiously he peered inside. It was dark in there, but he thought he could make out the outline of a table, some chairs and a sofa. A drawing room? He rested the rifle against the wall, lifted the window the rest of the way. His two minutes must be up by now, he thought. *But just let me get inside the house before the next guard comes by . . .*

He climbed silently into the drawing room, pulled the rifle in behind him, and let the window back down into its original position. Now all he had to do was find out where Ortega was sleeping without waking the rest of the house up.

That made him think of Rocco. Was that shotgun-carrying bastard here? Maybe. He'd have to find out somehow. He chewed thoughtfully at his bottom lip. This wasn't going to be a straightforward job at all. Still, he'd do his best, just like always. And more often than not, his best was damned good.

He waited a moment, crouched behind the sofa as he listened to the second of the three guards slowly walking past outside. How long it would take them to realize they were one man short O'Brien didn't know, but he hoped it would be long enough.

When the guard was out of earshot, he relaxed, stood up and moved across to the door.

He listened at one of the panels, heard nothing from the other side. He held his breath as he opened the door a fraction. He looked out into the entrance hall.

It was wide, wider than O'Brien's room back at the Palace Hotel in Tombstone, and lit by forty glowing candles that were strung along an eight-stemmed chandelier. There were oil paintings on the walls, small marble statuettes on elegant little tables. O'Brien opened the door wider, went through it and closed it behind him. He didn't relax for a moment.

From somewhere to his left came muted talk and laughter. He guessed that was where Ortega's other gunmen were quartered, someplace near the kitchen at the back of the house.

He turned right, away from the sound. His footsteps were lost in thick red carpet. He went to the foot of a wide staircase, looked up it with lips compressed and rifle aimed and ready. He tried the first step, then the second. The third one creaked just a little, but not too much. Then the fourth, the fifth, and so on all the way to the top.

There he stopped abruptly. Sitting in a straight-backed chair, chin resting on his chest and face covered by a sombrero, sat a man with a Peacemaker in a holster on his left hip. He had the back of the chair against the wall and his feet were swinging in mid-air. He was also snoring.

O'Brien let out a sigh of relief. He waited a moment, wiped his forehead, then moved forward quietly. When he was close enough, he put the Winchester down and took out the stolen Remington .44. It was in a fair condition, although a little scratched along the barrel. He pointed it at the sleeping figure, and with his left hand, abruptly clamped the guard's mouth.

The man struggled, let out a muffled oath, looked up through red-rimmed eyes. When he saw the seven-and-a-half inch barrel of the gun, his eyes went wider still. Then he looked at O'Brien, scared.

'Good, good,' O'Brien told him in a whisper. 'You didn't go for your gun. Wise man. Now listen, friend, where's Ortega's room?'

The Mexican shook his head, but O'Brien tightened his grip on the guard's mouth. 'Where's Ortega's room?' he repeated.

He watched the guard's bloodshot eyes. They were still wide and frightened, but they managed to flicker to a point over O'Brien's shoulder. O'Brien looked that way. The corridor was long and wide. There were four doors leading off it, all set in the right-hand wall.

O'Brien gave the guard a cold smile. 'Which room? At the end?'

A restricted nod.

'Good. Now let me tell you, *amigo*. If you're lying to me I'm going to come back here and blow your balls off, got it?'

Another nod.

O'Brien said: 'Is Rocco here?'

The man shook his head.

O'Brien sighed. 'All right.'

He brought the man forward gently until all four chair legs were on the floor. Then he used the barrel of the Remington on the back of the man's head, holding him in the chair as he slumped forward, unconscious. He, too, would wake up in the morning with a headache.

O'Brien put the Remington away, took up the rifle and moved quietly down the corridor. He paused at every door, putting his ear to the wood, listening. He heard no sounds. At the fourth door he could hear heavy, regular breathing, a cough, then the continuation of the breathing. So Ortega was in there, was he? Well, this was it, then.

★ ★ ★

He licked his lips, twisted the door handle, opened it and went inside . . .

6

O'Brien closed the door behind him, stood there with his back to it for a moment, holding his breath. He set the rifle against the wall, then moved across to the bed, saw the figure huddled beneath the sheets, and reached down.

As he had done with the guard in the corridor, he clamped his hand over Ortega's mouth to stifle any cry, and even as the man in the bed came awake with a start, O'Brien reached across with his free hand and turned up the bedside lamp.

The room came to life then, and he saw rich curtains and lace, more of those elegant little tables, a bureau, chairs, a thick carpet, a crystal decanter and glasses, a shelf with a few papers and books on it . . . and the man in the bed.

Except that the man was a woman.

Her dark skin and deep brown eyes showed her Mexican heritage. Her hair shone blue-black and was cut short like a boy's, but there was nothing boyish about the figure beneath her plain woolen nightgown. She was in her late twenties, and the most beautiful woman O'Brien had seen in a long, long while.

They stared at each other in the golden glow of the lamp for what seemed to O'Brien like an age. There was no fear in her dark eyes, just spirit.

O'Brien thought, *What the hell am I going to do now?*

Something had gone wrong somewhere along the line. He had to silence her somehow, and get away. But how? He was not above striking women, but the women in question had to deserve it otherwise O'Brien couldn't bring himself to do it. And anyway, who would want to bruise a face this beautiful?

The sight of her had thrown him completely. But then he knew what to do. The girl decided for him. She bit him.

He stepped back from the bed, turned and reached for the rifle just as she began to yell.

Then he was back in the corridor and racing along the carpet to the head of the stairs. He was dimly aware of her footsteps behind him, but gave her no thought. The important thing now was to get the hell out of here in one piece and re-think his strategy.

As he began to descend the stairs, five men burst into the hallway below. They were all cut from the same cloth: for all O'Brien knew they might have been among the men who'd invaded the Lost Life with Rocco all those weeks before. They had guns drawn and a couple of them started firing as soon as they saw him.

O'Brien threw himself back up the stairs, landed belly-down on the carpet and fired the rifle. It made a loud boom and chipped wood from the banister rail. The five gunmen below scuttled for cover. In the confined space, the noise of gunfire left their ears ringing.

O'Brien drew a bead on a thin American and blew him backwards. The gunman left a red mark on the wall when he fell to the floor.

More bullets ripped chunks out of the wall above O'Brien. Instinctively he flinched, returned fire without effect. Then O'Brien heard a voice above the gunfire, and chanced a look up the corridor. The girl was standing there, the light from her room outlining her figure through the nightgown. O'Brien had a chance to admire her legs before he realized she was holding a tiny pistol in both hands. After that he noticed two things. One was that the pistol was pointed his way. The other was that she held it rock steady, and he knew she would use it if she had to.

'Throw down that rifle!' she yelled in English.

The shooting from below started to fade out as the gunmen became aware of her voice. Soon it was replaced by heavy silence. O'Brien looked from her dark eyes to the barrel of the gun. It was a gambler's gun, a derringer, and even though it was of small caliber and good for close-up work alone, she was near enough to him to do some serious damage.

He slid the rifle away from him and slowly got onto his knees. He didn't have to be told to reach across with his right hand and take the Remington from its holster by his fingertips. This weapon he slid away from him, too.

As the gunmen below started up the stairs, the girl looked at the guard sitting at the far end of the corridor. 'Pedro!' The guard did not move. 'Pedro?'

One of the gunmen from below passed O'Brien and examined the guard. 'He's been cold-cocked, Miss Ortega.'

O'Brien studied the girl with renewed interest. She must be Ortega's daughter.

Oh boy, have I messed up.

He became aware that she was returning his scrutiny.

'Stand up,' she said. She had a deep, authoritative voice. Obviously used to giving orders and having them obeyed. O'Brien stood up. He held his hands high, uncomfortably aware of the many guns now trained on him.

'Cole's dead,' someone shouted from below.

'Who are you?' the girl asked.

'No-one you'd know,' O'Brien replied.

One of the gunmen struck him, hard, in the small of the back. He sagged, managed to straighten up again.

'Can you tell me why I shouldn't have you hung?' the girl demanded.

'Give me some time,' O'Brien replied. 'I'll think of something.'

He prepared himself for another blow, but none came.

The girl seemed to realize what she must look like, standing there. She said, 'Take him downstairs, into the drawing room. Don't harm him — yet. I will be down in a moment.' She turned and padded back to her room.

One of the gunmen yanked O'Brien around and pushed him hard. He stumbled down three stairs, caught his balance and walked the rest of the way. In the entrance hall two more men were carrying the dead man away. Frightened Mexican staff were watching from a door at the far end of the hall. Someone was already washing the blood off the wall.

O'Brien was taken into the drawing room and thrust roughly into a ladder-back chair. Someone kept a gun on him while another lit some lamps. At any other time O'Brien might have thought the room was cozy, but not right now. He did notice the portrait over the fireplace, though. It was of an old man, who had fuzzy hair scraped across his domelike head and the same brown eyes as the girl upstairs. O'Brien knew it was a portrait of Jose Ortega.

There was an ornate clock over the mantel. The time was one-twenty. O'Brien suddenly thought of Gleason, waiting out there in the night. He must have heard the gunfire. But what would he do? Hang back, wait and see if he could do some good when the right moment came along, or just come bursting in, hoping for the best?

Another gunman came through the front door, supporting the poncho-clad guard O'Brien had dealt with out in the garden. The guard was shaking his head and dragging his feet. A few minutes later, the girl came into the room. She had dressed in a white linen blouse and wine-red skirt. There was nothing fancy about the clothes at all, but there was something in the way she wore them that held O'Brien's interest. She stood by the fireplace, watching him. She looked grim, and beneath her blouse her breasts rose and fell to the tempo of her angry breathing.

'What were you trying to do here?' she asked after a while.

O'Brien shrugged.

'Were you sent here by someone?'

'No.'

'You're lying,' she bluffed. 'Who sent you? Was it Rocco?' She made the name sound like a curse.

O'Brien raised his eyebrows in surprise. 'I wasn't sent by anyone,' he replied. 'I have some business with *Senor* Ortega.'

'You are a liar,' she said. 'How can you have business with my father? My father is dead, *senor*.'

O'Brien's face went blank with shock. She saw it and frowned. 'Who are you?' she asked again.

'My name — '

At that moment there was a disturbance at the front door and the girl swished across the room to see what the matter was. O'Brien tensed. There were two men in the room, and both of them were watching the entrance hall. If he timed it right, he might be able to dive through the window and lose himself in the night.

But then he saw what had caused the disturbance and sagged a little. Three men were herding Gleason into the house. There was a cut on his forehead and he was limping on his left foot. One of the guards gave him a push and he stumbled forward, falling to his knees. He groaned and got back on his feet awkwardly. The girl threw a look at O'Brien. O'Brien looked away.

Gleason faced the three men who had brought him in. The blood running down his face looked like gaudy war paint. But he drew himself up and his fists folded. As he stared at the men there was no mistaking the challenge in his eyes. 'Come on, then,' he said quietly. 'Any time you want.'

One of the three men swaggered forward. He reached out to take hold of Gleason's shoulder, but Gleason batted his hand away and lashed out with his right fist. The gunman gave a squeal of surprise and staggered back, nose bloody. Gleason limped forward but was too slow to follow it up. The second of the three men stepped forward and punched him in the stomach. Gleason bent over but did not go down.

'Miguel!'

One of the men turned. '*Si, senorita?*'

'Bring that man here. Who is he? Where did you find him?'

The man called Miguel took hold of

Gleason's shoulder and pushed him across the hallway. 'He was in the grounds at the back of the house, *senorita*. Ramirez saw him and the three of us rushed him.'

The girl dismissed him and went back to the fireplace. Gleason, standing in the doorway, saw O'Brien and his eyes lit up briefly. 'Carter!'

'Sit down, *senor*,' the girl told him. She sighed heavily. 'Are there any more of your friends outside?'

Both men said nothing.

'I am Catarina Ortega,' the girl said. 'Everything that was my father's now belongs to me. Any 'business' you had with him is now my concern.' Her eyes fell to O'Brien. 'You are not common thieves, that much is obvious. So what are you? And who?'

O'Brien shrugged. 'I am Carter O'Brien,' he said, 'and this is Major John Gleason.'

The girl's eyes narrowed. 'Gleason is dead,' she said uncertainly.

'Is that what Rocco told you?' O'Brien asked.

Her eyes flared at the mention of his name. She studied them carefully. 'I am aware of the circumstances surrounding my father's purchase of the Lost Life,' she said quietly. 'If you are who you say you are, where are your friends?'

Gleason said, 'They're dead.'

Again there was a long pause before she said more. 'You came here to kill my father, is that it?'

O'Brien said, honestly, 'I don't know.'

'I think you did, *senor*.'

'We'll never know now, will we? When did he die, anyway?'

Catarina Ortega did not reply. Instead she asked, 'How can it be that you survived the San Felipe desert?'

'God was with us,' O'Brien said softly.

She threw a glance at the clock on the mantel. Again she gave a heavy sigh. To one of the guards she said, 'Take them down to the cellar. I want a guard kept there for the rest of the night.' The man nodded.

'What are you going to do with us?'

Gleason inquired.

Catarina Ortega smiled. It was not meant to be reassuring. 'My father's enemies are now my enemies,' she replied. 'I will think of something before sunrise.'

They were taken away. Through the house they were led, into the large and spotless kitchen, where one guard threw back a mat and lifted a trapdoor. They were pushed roughly toward the opening in the floor, forced down the narrow wooden steps into the Stygian blackness below. When they reached the bottom they turned and looked up at the square of light. One of the guards said, 'Remember that someone will be up here at all times, my friends, just hoping you will give him the excuse he needs to kill you.'

Then the trapdoor was lowered and the darkness swallowed them.

Cautiously they felt their way about. Somewhere not too far away they heard the scuttling and squealing of rats. They found boxes and sat down. Gleason asked O'Brien what had happened and O'Brien told him.

Afterwards, Gleason said, 'The minute I heard the shooting I came running. From what I could hear most of the action was taking place at the front of the house, so I snuck 'round to the back and came over the wall. Trouble was, I twisted my ankle when I landed. I was just about to move when I got spotted.' He muttered a curse and began to apologize again.

'Save it. Try and get some rest. When they come back for us in the morning, we'd better be ready to grab the first chance we get to bust out of here.'

Gleason whispered, 'You reckon she'll have us killed?'

O'Brien paused before replying. 'She's her daddy's little girl, I reckon. Chances are she might just kill us *herself*.'

They dozed for the rest of the night. At eight o'clock the trapdoor was opened and they rose, blinking up at the shaft of dusty light. Someone said, 'All right, come on up.'

They started up the steps, O'Brien in the lead. When they came up into the kitchen, they paused for a moment as their eyes grew used to the light again. Then they were pushed back through the house and into the drawing room.

Catarina Ortega sat waiting for them. She was dressed in a khaki shirt and matching pants. She studied them for a long time. They stood before her, dusty and rumpled. The blood had dried on Gleason's face and his ankle was better. After a moment, Catarina Ortega flicked a glance at one of the two rifle-wielding guards in the room.

'Charro, go fetch a bowl of water for Major Gleason's head, and tell Anna to prepare breakfast for them both.'

'*Si, senorita.*'

When the guard had gone she stared at them and a smile O'Brien didn't like the look of played across her lips. 'A drink gentlemen?' she asked.

O'Brien said, 'Whiskey, thanks.'

'Major?'

Gleason looked uncomfortably at

O'Brien, then nodded. 'The same.'

After she had poured them their drinks, she sat opposite them again. She looked at the remaining guard. 'Leave us, Mano. Tell Charro to knock before he enters.'

Then they were left alone, and O'Brien smelled the whiskey. It seemed all right. He tried it. It was good. Catarina Ortega watched him with amusement shining in her eyes. When she made no move to speak, O'Brien asked, 'When?'

She lifted an eyebrow. 'When what, senor?'

'When do you stop playing games and have us killed?'

She laughed. 'Are you that eager to die?'

There was a knock at the door and one of the guards, Charro, came in, carrying a bowl of steaming water and a cloth. He set the bowl down on the table at Gleason's side and left without a word. Gleason set his glass aside and started to wash the dark, crusted blood from his face. Catarina Ortega watched him dispassionately.

'Gentlemen, you came here for one purpose: revenge. Quite rightly, you blamed my father for your misfortunes, but you were cheated. My father has been dead for almost two months.' She looked from one to the other of them. 'However, I am willing to offer you the revenge you seek.'

Gleason frowned. 'How?'

Her dark eyes turned hard. 'By giving you the chance to kill Nathan Rocco.'

She seemed pleased at the surprise on their faces.

'Allow me to explain,' she said. 'The last time I saw Rocco was two months ago, when he rode in one afternoon to report that the Lost Life was ours, and that you, major, and your men, were dead. He had been drinking heavily, but my father was so pleased with him that he allowed him to stay here at the *hacienda* for a few days, by way of a reward.

'But that evening he made certain ... advances toward me. My father heard the commotion and came to investigate. When he saw what was happening, he struck Rocco and told him to get out. Before I knew it, Rocco took his knife and stabbed my father in the chest.'

Her voice did not waver. She told the story as if she were reading it from a very old and boring book.

'My father was dead within the hour, by which time Rocco and his men were long gone.'

In the ensuing silence, they heard flies buzzing at the open window. O'Brien said, 'So you want Rocco dead, and you're willing to let us have a crack at him because you know we want him dead too.'

She inclined her head. 'It seems fairly obvious to me that Rocco has returned to the Lost Life. No-one else knows of its location, so he would feel safe from pursuit there. Of course, I have a number of options open to me. I could send a small army into the Sierra de San Pedro, but they might spend weeks searching for him without success. Then again, they might find him straight away and throw in with him because of the fortune in silver of which he is now in possession. But you . . . gentlemen . . . you both know the location of the Lost Life, and I think I can rely on you to do your best to deal with Rocco or die trying.'

'What's in it for us?' O'Brien asked straight away. 'Apart from the satisfaction of getting even with Rocco, that is?'

She lifted one eyebrow. 'You get the chance to stay alive,' she said simply.

O'Brien shook his head. 'It's not enough,' he replied. Before she could speak, he said, 'We wanted revenge, sure, but we also wanted the Lost Life. It's ours by right and your father stole it from us.'

The ghost of a smile played across her lips. 'You have nerve,' she said.

'Yes, ma'am. Especially when I know I'm right.'

Her smile stayed where it was. 'I hate to remind you, *senor*, but you're in no position to bargain.'

O'Brien sighed heavily. 'Then if you don't mind me saying so, *senorita*, you can damned well go to hell.'

Her eyes flashed. Before she could reply, O'Brien interrupted. 'What you've got to consider, ma'am, is how much you want Rocco dead. Now, you're a sensible young lady, and I figure you loved your daddy a whole lot. And, like you said, the major and me know the country and we want Rocco as bad as you. Still, if you don't think your daddy's memory is worth the cost of the Lost Life . . . '

'*Senor* O'Brien . . . '

O'Brien held out his empty glass. 'Another, *por favor*.'

The girl colored, but managed to hold down her temper. She snatched O'Brien's glass away from him and took it to the drinks table. She spent a long time facing the wall and pouring the drink. When she turned back to them, she had regained her composure. As she handed him the glass, she said quietly,

'All right. The Lost Life is yours.'

O'Brien tasted the whiskey. 'Thank you, *senorita*.'

'There's just one thing,' Gleason said, waiting until the girl was seated again. 'We don't *want* the Lost Life.'

O'Brien nearly choked up.

'So we'll sell it to you,' Gleason continued calmly. 'For one hundred thousand dollars.'

The girl colored again. 'You . . . you are insufferable, *senor!* I will not — '

'I think Mr. O'Brien and I agree on this, *senorita*,' Gleason said firmly. 'We have no desire to stay in Mexico, and would be much happier allowing you to purchase the Lost Life from us. Once we conclude the deal, it will be our intention to pay the mine one last visit, and when we come down again, Nathan Rocco will be as dead as a doornail.'

She did not reply for a long time. O'Brien could see her thinking it over. Then she said, 'One hundred thousand dollars is a lot of money, *senor*. Perhaps — '

161

'We won't dicker with you, *senorita*,' O'Brien cut in. 'That's the price we are asking, and that's the price you'll pay.'

Again she said, 'You have nerve.'

O'Brien nodded. 'I thank you for the compliment.'

Gleason, sensing that they might be pushing her too far, said, 'Well, at least let's listen to the *senorita's* offer.'

She gave him a cold smile. 'Fifty thousand,' she said softly.

Before O'Brien could object, Gleason said, 'Seventy-five.'

'Sixty.'

'Seventy.'

Gleason met her gaze. She could see in his eyes that he would go no lower. After a while, she nodded and said, 'Agreed. Seventy thousand dollars. The money will be waiting for you upon your return. But I will demand proof that Nathan Rocco is dead.'

O'Brien smiled easily. 'We'll take half the money now, and the rest when we get back,' he amended. 'As for Rocco . . . you'll have your proof.'

She nodded, tight-lipped.

'We'll need guns, decent horses, supplies for a month,' O'Brien said. She nodded again. 'We'll also need some men. They'll have to be fighters, and I only want the ones you trust completely. I don't want to have to watch my back all the time.'

'You shall have them,' she said, half to herself. 'How many?'

O'Brien looked at Gleason. Gleason nodded, remembering the last time they had set out after Rocco, eight years before. O'Brien said, 'Nine.'

'I will see to it,' she said. There was a knock at the door, and a young Mexican girl stepped into the room and announced that breakfast was ready. 'Thank you, Anna. Gentlemen?'

They rose, but before leaving, O'Brien said, 'We'll leave at first light tomorrow. Can you arrange everything by then?'

'I can.'

'And the money?'

'It will be ready,' Catarina Ortega replied testily.

O'Brien nodded. 'And one other thing,' he said.

'Yes?'

His eyes met hers and held them. 'Can we trust you not to double-cross us the minute we get back?'

She did not speak straight away. And then, at last, she smiled. 'You can,' she told him.

O'Brien nodded again. He believed her.

7

After breakfast, they were shown to two bright guest rooms. Baths had been prepared for them, and O'Brien spent a long time soaking. When at last he climbed out of the tub, he discovered that his old clothes had been taken and replaced with fresh ones. Later in the day he was given a weapons belt, a Cavalry Colt and a Winchester. Four boxes of .44/40 ammunition were left discreetly on the bedside cabinet by a silent old manservant.

During the afternoon there was a knock at the door, and a tall, slim man of indeterminate age asked O'Brien to follow him. Gleason stood at the tall man's side. They were led through the house and out into a courtyard at the rear, where they were shown a string of horses and asked to make their selection. Gleason chose a spirited mustang, O'Brien a somewhat calmer piebald. The tall man nodded. 'They will be ready for you at first light, senores.'

They did not see Catarina Ortega again that day. That evening they dined alone, but were shown every courtesy by the servants. They briefly discussed their ideas for dealing with Rocco, but since there was still too much they didn't know, their plans remained sketchy. By the time he fell into bed that night, O'Brien had accounted for much of Ortega's whiskey and tobacco. Not surprisingly, he slept well.

The next time they saw Catarina Ortega was at sun-up the following morning. The sky was just beginning to brighten with the promise of a new day, and as they stepped out into the courtyard, their shadows were stretched long across the cobbles. She nodded briefly as they climbed into their saddles.

The nine men she had chosen sat their ponies in a line facing them. They ranged in age from their mid-twenties to early forties. They were all Mexican, and all well-armed. There was no telling what was going through their minds as they sat staring blankly ahead.

Catarina Ortega turned to them and told them what she expected of them. O'Brien, who spoke Spanish more or less fluently, approved of what she had to say. As she finished, the sun began to rise like a swollen ball of blood in the east.

Then she turned her attention back to O'Brien and Gleason. Slowly, she walked across to them, looking up into their faces as she approached. Her own face was as blank as those of her men. O'Brien couldn't even guess what she might be thinking.

She handed a bulky envelope up to Gleason. 'Thirty-five thousand dollars,' she said calmly. The other half will be waiting for you upon your return.'

Gleason touched the brim of his hat. 'Thank you, *senorita*.' He stashed the envelope in his saddlebag.

She allowed her dark eyes to flicker briefly across the nine men sitting quietly on the other side of the courtyard. 'I have told them to consider you both in command of this expedition.'

O'Brien nodded briskly. 'We will see you again, *senorita*,' he said. 'And soon. You can count on it.'

'We shall see,' she said softly. Again she studied them, her dark face impossible to read. At last she nodded, as though satisfied. 'Goodbye.'

They nodded to her, then rode out, keeping up a steady, mile-eating pace until both the *hacienda* and Calamajué were left behind them.

When they were out in open country, O'Brien threw a glance over his shoulder. The nine Mexicans rode in silence, two abreast, with the guard who had brought Gleason a bowl of water the previous day, Charro, at their head. There was no conversation between them, and this worried O'Brien. He had no doubt that they would obey

Catarina's instructions — they were her most trusted men, after all — but he knew it was important to establish a more personal relationship with them. Before too long he was going to have to fight alongside them, and he had to know how much they could be relied upon.

That night they camped on the trail and O'Brien posted two guards, with instructions that they be relieved by two more at midnight. The remaining Mexicans kept firmly to themselves on the far side of the campfire. O'Brien and Gleason drank coffee in silence for a long while before O'Brien called Charro across from where he played dice with the others.

He was a big, broad man with high cheekbones and a wide, broken nose. As he approached them, he studied them with dark, suspicious eyes. '*Si, senor?*'

'Sit down, Charro,' O'Brien said in Spanish. 'Coffee?'

Charro shook his head.

O'Brien said, 'If I wanted to hire some men, just ordinary manual workers, where would be the best place to go?'

Charro considered this briefly. 'Miramar,' he said after a moment.

'Where's that?'

The big Mexican looked off into the night. 'About ten miles to the north.'

O'Brien did not speak at once, and Charro wondered whether or not he should get up and leave them. But then O'Brien said, 'Smoke?'

Charro nodded, accepting the Durham sack O'Brien held out to him. 'Are we going to Miramar, *senor*?'

O'Brien nodded. 'If Rocco wanted some men to work the Lost Life, chances are he'd have gone there first. When we get there we'll make some enquiries and see what we can find out.'

'And then we go to the Lost Life?' Charro asked expectantly.

'Yes.'

'And we kill Rocco?'

'If we don't bring him back to hang.'

Charro smiled, quite suddenly. It was not pleasant. 'I will kill him myself,' he said venomously. 'Twenty years I worked for *Senor* Ortega. Twenty years.' He shook his head, studying O'Brien through dangerous eyes. 'I will kill him for the sorrow he has brought to the *senorita*. I swear it.'

O'Brien struck a lucifer and lit Charro's cigarette. 'We'll see,' he said casually. 'All right, Charro. Everyone up at six in the morning. The sooner we reach Miramar, the sooner we can start out after Rocco.'

'It will be done, *senor*.' The Mexican stood up and O'Brien watched him rejoin the others, then turned to study Gleason's face, stained orange by the dancing flames.

'Well, one thing's for sure,' he said quietly. 'We can count on *him*, anyway.'

O'Brien smelled the sea before he saw it.

They had ridden easily all morning but still his shirt clung uncomfortably to his body. And then he began to catch the scent of salt on the faint, warm breeze and when they topped a ridge they saw Miramar scattered in the valley below them, a cluster of white-washed adobes overlooking the Gulf of California. O'Brien called a halt and waved Charro up front.

'*Si, senor?*'

'I want you and three men to ride down and see what you can find out,' O'Brien told him. Charro nodded and wheeled his horse back to the others. He rattled off three names and three riders cut away from the group. Charro touched the brim of his sombrero as they galloped off along the trail toward town.

O'Brien would have preferred to go with them, but he and Gleason had agreed the previous night that they had to make the Mexicans feel as much a part of this mission as they were, otherwise resentment might start building up. Certainly the three men Charro had selected seemed happy to have been chosen.

The rest of them dismounted and loosened the cinches on their mounts. They found what little shade they could and sprawled out in it. O'Brien watched the sun glinting off the blue waters below. He didn't often get the chance to see the sea, and it fascinated him.

He felt the Mexicans watching him. Although their employer had chosen to trust the two *gringos*, they were still uncertain. O'Brien would have to earn their trust in some way.

Charro and his men rode in a couple of hours later, the big Mexican reining in where O'Brien and Gleason sat beneath the patchy shade of a Joshua tree. 'I have some information, *senores*.'

'Okay, Charro, spill it.'

Charro slid down from the saddle and uncapped his canteen. He drank from it, poured a little into his sombrero and held it to his horse's muzzle. 'About six weeks ago, a Yaqui came to town and hired fifteen laborers. We spoke to many people, but none of them could tell us what job they had been hired for, or where they were taken when they left town. But there are many unhappy families in Miramar, senores, for not one of the fifteen laborers has been heard from since.'

'A Yaqui,' Gleason said thoughtfully. He looked at O'Brien, lifting his eyebrows. 'Alvarez?'

'That's what I was wondering.'

'You know Alvarez?' Charro asked.

'We met him once,' O'Brien said mildly. 'And we'd like to meet him again.'

'So Rocco's got his workers,' Gleason said, rising.

O'Brien rose with him. 'Fifteen innocent men,' he said. 'I just hope none of 'em get caught in the crossfire, if it comes to a fight.' He focused on the men around him. 'All right, you fellers, let's ride.'

'The Lost Life?' Charro asked hopefully.

O'Brien threw one final glance at the sea. 'The Lost Life,' he replied softly.

They rode hard, northwest across vast flatlands.

In two days they covered better than forty miles, and on the third day they reined in to stare up at the towering blue peaks scratching the sky six miles away.

O'Brien's eyes traced the lines of the Sierra. The last time he had stared at them he had believed his life to be over. It still could be, if things went wrong when they reached the Lost Life. But at least now he had a gun and the element of surprise. That had to count for something.

He glanced across at Gleason, whose blue eyes were fixed straight ahead. O'Brien knew he was re-living their ordeal in the desert. It was a nightmare that would haunt them both for a long time to come. O'Brien sighed and turned in the saddle. The Mexicans watched him with faces that were unreadable.

'From here on in, we use outriders,' he said. 'Lopez, Colquin — I want one of you on either flank, about half a mile ahead. You see anything I ought to know about, hightail it back here, you got it?'

The two Mexicans nodded, their dark faces serious but eager. They broke away from the main group and kicked their horses into a gallop.

O'Brien then turned his attention to the others. 'It could be that Rocco will have some of his men out in the hills, patrolling. I don't think that's likely, but I want you to keep your guns handy, just in case.' He glanced at Gleason again. 'You ready?'

Gleason nodded.

They urged their horses forward.

Clouds, driven by a faint, dry breeze, moved across the sky, throwing dark shadows across the wide desert floor. It was still hot, even this late in the season, but tension made them sweat, as well.

By mid-afternoon they were in the foothills, winding their way in single file along a narrow, rocky trail that led gently upward. Gradually rock and sand gave way to sparse grass and ocotillo. During the afternoon, O'Brien sent two men to relieve the outriders, but didn't call a halt until early evening. After they had posted guards, they settled to a cold supper, washed down by mugs of hot coffee to combat the chill of approaching night.

'Is the Lost Life very far now, senores?' Charro asked after they had finished eating.

O'Brien looked at Gleason. Gleason shrugged. 'It's difficult to say. Maybe another day's ride.'

'Then we attack soon,' Charro said eagerly. A few of the Mexicans made sounds of approval.

'That depends,' O'Brien replied. 'When we get close enough, I'll go in and have a look 'round before we start making any plans.'

'Will you need some company when you go, senor?'

'Thanks, Charro, but I'd better go alone.'

Conversation settled into more general matters. As the evening wore on, a couple of Mexicans bedded down, a couple more occupied themselves with a game of cards. Gleason lit up a cigar and O'Brien rolled a cigarette, enjoying the stillness of the night. The showdown was coming. Soon.

The next morning they were off before the sun had risen, O'Brien and Charro riding ahead to scout the land. O'Brien had committed Gleason's map to memory, but there was still much of the Sierra with which he was unfamiliar. Time and again he scanned the terrain for landmarks, but always without success.

At noon they called a halt to spell the horses. Keeping in the shade, the men rinsed their mouths with tepid water and dampened the sweatbands on their hats before riding on. They kept to a cautious walk and held their rifles ready across their saddle horns, just in case.

But the outriders saw no-one. Even so, O'Brien did not allow himself to relax. Repeatedly he led his men around wide, exposed spaces rather than cut straight across. This close to the Lost

Life, they couldn't afford to take chances.

Sometime in the late afternoon, they came to a small pool of water kept cool by the shadow of a large slab of granite, and O'Brien decided to make camp. By the time they had posted guards, seen to the horses and found some old, dry twigs to make a smokeless fire over which they could heat coffee and beans, the sky had turned deep blue and the sun began melting into the horizon.

'We are close to the canyon now, senor?' one of the Mexicans asked as they ate.

O'Brien nodded. 'Less than three miles away, how I figure it.'

'Then you are going to look around tonight?' Charro asked. When O'Brien nodded again, he said, 'You are sure you do not want some company?'

'I'm sure, Charro, but I appreciate the offer.'

O'Brien spent a restless evening waiting for nightfall. It was a restlessness that communicated itself to the others. There was little conversation.

Tonight, the men seemed to prefer their own company. At last, O'Brien got to his feet, reaching down to slide his Winchester from its sheath. He checked his watch — it was a little after midnight.

'I'm going a-foot, John. Don't know how long it'll take, but I'll give three owlhoots before I come back in, so make sure whoever's standing guard don't get too trigger-happy.'

Gleason nodded. 'Good luck.'

A few of the Mexicans mumbled farewells as O'Brien slipped away into the night. The sky was clear and the moon full. The whole area was bathed in silver, O'Brien just a shadow as he moved from cover to cover. He moved northwest, guided by the distant stars. Small animal sounds came to his ears. Every so often branches shook as birds left their nests, and bushes shivered with the passing of small, nocturnal animals. In the distance, a wolf howled. A short time later, he heard others.

O'Brien trotted along in silence,

hoping to Christ he was heading in the right direction. He moved on through the night with all the silence of a forbidden thought. He stopped once to check the time. He had been moving for little more than an hour. He looked off into the darkness, hoping for a clue to point him in the right direction.

Nothing.

After a while, he came to a patch of open ground where a jagged needle of rock, rising from a jumble of boulders on the far side like a church spire, stirred a memory inside him. He came to a halt and peered into the shadows. He couldn't see much, but just about heard the faint liquid sounds of a running stream. He started to move again, until he felt the hard earth beneath him begin to slope downward. Looking up, he saw the bare branches of cypress trees clawing at the sky. Boulders threw great blankets of shadow all around him.

At last he knew where he was. It had taken him almost two hours, but he was here at last. The Lost Life.

It was a strange feeling, coming back. His mouth went dry. The memory of everything that had led him to this moment suddenly came back, making him feel light-headed. With an effort he forced himself to concentrate on the business at hand.

He dodged from one scrap of cover to the next, keeping his eyes open for any guards who might be patrolling. As far as he could recall, he was approaching the canyon from the far end. From here he would be able to look down into it and get a picture of how things had changed since he was last here. Any information he could pick up now would determine what they did next.

He saw a faint orange glow about fifteen feet away — firelight. He was almost at the rim of the canyon. Then he heard another sound, the sound of a man walking through the dry, white grass that powdered the rim. He drifted back into the thick shadows.

The guard walked past quickly. He

wasn't expecting trouble so he wasn't looking for it. He was rubbing his arms beneath his thick poncho. O'Brien let him go. His eyes stabbed the darkness, but he saw no-one else. He moved forward.

The canyon looked different from above. It was about sixty yards long and twenty yards wide, its walls towering thirty feet in height. Here was the corner where he and Morton had fought, there the one where he and the others had been held prisoner before being taken down and left to die in the desert.

In the center of the canyon a large fire had been lit. A few men stood or sat around it, talking. At this distance, O'Brien could not hear what they were saying. A few others were wrapped in bedrolls a short way off. A quick headcount told him that there were fifteen of them. There were a couple of tents nearby. Of Rocco and Alvarez there was no sign.

The corner where he and Morton

had fought had been turned into a remuda. It held twenty-six horses. Next to the horses, O'Brien saw the huddled figures of several men. These must be the workers Alvarez had picked up in Miramar. In the weak firelight he noticed how poorly they were dressed. Their thin cotton shirts and woolen trousers were torn and stained, no protection at all from the chill high-country nights. There were twelve of them. Maybe the other three were dead. The way it looked at the moment, they were the lucky ones.

O'Brien scanned the rest of the canyon. Scaffolding had been erected along one stretch of the wall so that the higher veins could be reached. A little further along was a large stack of supplies packed in crates and cartons. Almost opposite was a pile of picks and shovels, and a large pile of crates covered with a tarpaulin. Mined silver?

Then O'Brien caught a movement out of the corner of one eye and turned his attention back to the campfire. Two men had stepped out of the smaller tent.

Rocco and Alvarez!

O'Brien's teeth clenched. If he had been anything less than the professional he was, he'd have blown their brains out there and then. As it was, he just watched them join the men by the fire and take coffee with them.

He slid back into the darkness and cat-footed around the canyon rim. He found four guards, either patrolling or hunkering by small fires. There was one more guard by the box canyon's narrow entrance. They neither saw nor heard him pass them by.

'So that's about the size of it,' O'Brien said in conclusion.

It had taken him just over an hour to find his way back to camp where Gleason and the others had been dozing lightly.

As he spoke, he counted off the points with his fingers. 'I've told you the layout of the place. Rocco's got at least twenty-one men with him, including

Alvarez. Four men guard the rim of the canyon, another guards the entrance.'

Gleason said nothing. His face was difficult to read in the weak fire glow. 'We can't risk shooting any of those workers,' he said. 'We have no quarrel with them. So we'll have to attack at first light, when we can see exactly what we're shooting at.'

O'Brien nodded. One of the Mexicans, a young man named Jorge, coughed to attract their attention. He was obviously embarrassed when all eyes turned to him. 'Then what exactly is the plan, *senores?* Forgive me if I appear to speak out of turn, but . . . I will fight those men willingly for what they have done to *Senorita* Ortega, but I will have no part in an ambush. The fight will have to be fair.'

'No-one's talking about ambushing them,' O'Brien replied. 'We'll give them the chance to surrender.'

'But do you think they will take it?'

'They'd be fools not to. We'll have them surrounded. But if I know Rocco, it'll come to shooting. He'll do exactly what he did the last time we had him surrounded, eight years ago — deliberately provoke a fight in order to escape in the confusion.'

'So the plan, *senores?*' Charro asked.

O'Brien looked at Gleason. 'Major?'

Gleason returned his smile. Then they got to work.

8

More than anything else right then, O'Brien wanted to sleep, and after they had agreed a plan and made sure everyone was familiar with it, he fell into his bedroll, exhausted. Rest was important right now. The showdown was just twenty-four hours away.

When he woke, the sun was high. He sat up and drank from his canteen, then grimaced. The water was warm.

A few of the others were busy cleaning their guns. Nobody spoke much, nobody laughed or smiled. At mid-day, they forced themselves to eat, but they barely tasted the food. As the sun climbed higher, the heat grew overpowering. Some of the Mexicans tried to sleep the afternoon away, the rest tried to concentrate on cards or dice. One even read from a small, dog-eared Bible.

At last the sun began its long descent

in the west. Around them, the Sierra was as quiet as the grave.

Night fell, but still they did not move. The hours seemed to drag past. They smoked, their eyes fixed on distant points as they remembered people and places they might never see again. It got so that when O'Brien called them to their feet at one a.m., they were almost glad to get moving, even though they knew they might not be coming back again when it was all over.

They saddled up and walked their horses away from the camp, riding in single file behind O'Brien and Gleason. Clouds hid the moon, so their progress was slow. The night was cold, and breath misted before their faces. At last they came to the clearing in which the needle of rock thrust up at the sky, and here they tethered their mounts. The animals would be near enough if they were needed, and far enough from the canyon that any sounds they might make wouldn't betray their riders.

They went the rest of the way on

foot. Nobody spoke. There was no need: everyone knew what was expected of them. When O'Brien judged they were close enough, he, Charro and two others split away from the main group. O'Brien pointed each man in a different direction, and watched them disappear into the darkness. Within the next quarter of an hour, four guards died soundlessly, their throats kissed by cold steel.

O'Brien made a circuit of the canyon rim, nodding his approval to the waiting Mexicans. They met up with the others again, and O'Brien nodded that the first part of the job was done. Gleason clapped him on the shoulder, then led six men away, leaving O'Brien where he was, with the remaining three. One of them handed him his rifle. They had fashioned slings for them, and O'Brien slipped his over one shoulder.

He led his men silently to the rim of the canyon. They hardly dared breathe for fear of attracting attention. Everything was as it had been the night before. Most of the gunmen were asleep. Two sat around the campfire, talking in low tones. They were about forty feet away.

O'Brien checked the time: it was nearly a quarter after two. Still too early to go into action. He signaled for the men with him to ease back into the brush.

It was hard work, perhaps the hardest job of all, to wait. They had to allow their minds to wander and yet stay alert at all times. Then, at three o'clock, O'Brien decided to move. This was the best time to take people unaware, the time when the human spirit was at its lowest. He took a lariat from his belt and lowered one end gently over the canyon rim, inch by inch, until it disappeared behind the shadows of the scaffolding fifteen feet below.

He ran the rest of the rope back into the darkness, until he found a heavy rock around which he secured his end. Rejoining the three Mexicans, he took another look at the two men around the fire. One was obviously asleep, the other stretched out, but propped up on one elbow. Fortunately, he was facing away from the scaffolding.

Well, then, this was it.

O'Brien took a grip on the rope and went over the side. He hung there for a moment, feeling the skin along his spine tingling, then began to lower himself, hand over hand, inch by inch, until his feet touched the wooden planks of the scaffold.

He lay flat on his belly. His palms were slick, his arms trembling. At last he looked up and motioned for the next man to descend.

He had deliberately chosen the three lightest men for this part of the plan. He turned his attention from the Mexican coming down the rope to the men stretched out by the fire. He hoped the crackling of the flames would drown any noise he or his men might make.

The Mexican came down into a crouch next to him, showing his white teeth in a relieved smile. O'Brien touched him on the shoulder, then beckoned for the next man, expecting at any moment to be discovered, and for all hell to break loose.

Gleason led his men along the canyon rim as silently as he could. Blood pounded in his ears. There was a time when this kind of situation would have brought out the best in him. Now it just reminded him of how old he was.

Suddenly there was a break in the cloud and the entire area was lit by a weird, pale glow.

Immediately Gleason stopped moving and went down onto his belly. The others followed suit. There was no sound, no movement, nothing.

He released his breath slowly, wiped a hand across his forehead, and got to his feet. A short way further along the rim, he indicated where two men should hide. Then they moved on, around the far end of the rim, where he positioned two more men, and went into hiding himself. He waved the last two Mexicans, Charro and Lopez, on into the night.

When the three Mexicans had joined

O'Brien on the scaffold, he led them along the planking until they came to the place where a ladder had been left propped up. By this time, both men by the campfire were asleep, no more than twenty feet away.

O'Brien had one foot on the ladder when one of the men sat up.

As one, they hugged the planking, holding their breath. Sweat trickled down O'Brien's cheek. The man by the fire got awkwardly to his feet, stumbled off a few paces, unbuttoned his pants and began to urinate. The splashes sounded loud in the stillness. After a while he yawned, scratched his backside, and came back to his bedroll. He lay down, rolled onto one side, and yawned again.

O'Brien lay absolutely still for another ten minutes. By the end of it nerves were twitching in his face, legs and hands. Slowly he turned his head to study the man. His chest rose and fell steadily. Good, he was asleep again. O'Brien allowed himself the faintest of sighs. He got up, and went down the ladder. The three

Mexicans were right behind him.

When they were on the canyon floor, O'Brien sent two of them into the shadows of some loose rock beneath the scaffold. He and the other Mexican, Jorge, scurried twenty feet along the silver-rich walls, hugging the darkness. They slid behind the crates of supplies. O'Brien slipped his rifle from his shoulder. He still couldn't believe they'd gotten this far without being discovered.

He felt Jorge watching him, turned and smiled briefly. Jorge smiled back, a tight, nervous smile. O'Brien checked his watch — it was a little before four a.m.

Just over an hour to first light.

The running stream covered any sounds Charro and Lopez might have made as they crept toward the man guarding the canyon entrance. A break in the cloud had shown them exactly where he was, and when darkness rolled back in, they were no more than six feet away from him.

The guard was a young man who

dreamed of getting rich and buying fancy clothes and weapons. He lounged against the smoothest rock, his Winchester propped against the wall close by. His mind was elsewhere as Charro and Lopez crept even closer.

Like lightning, Charro grabbed him, yanking him roughly out of the narrow defile. His hard right hand clamped the guard's mouth shut as Lopez came forward and stabbed him, twice, in the stomach. The guard went limp in Charro's arms.

The big Mexican dragged him away and dumped his body, while Lopez stepped in and took the Winchester from its place against the wall. Then they both retreated into the cover of some brush, to wait for dawn.

Once or twice men stirred in their sleep, coughed or got up to urinate. Horses whickered softly, a few men muttered odd words to themselves as they rolled over. O'Brien watched them through a gap in the crates.

The minutes went by slowly. O'Brien's

eyes felt wide and glassy. And then, gradually, the sky began to tinge with the faintest of reds. Shadows began to develop and grow. O'Brien checked the time again. It was two minutes past five in the morning. He glanced along the canyon to the scaffold. The shadows there were still thick. He couldn't see any trace of the Mexicans hiding there.

'*Rocco!*'

The shout tore through the still air. Almost at once O'Brien felt the tension beginning to rise. A ripple went through the sleeping men. They sat up quickly, most of them with guns in hand. If there was any doubt that they might be under attack, it was soon dispelled when Gleason, thirty feet above on the canyon rim, triggered a shot skyward.

The gunmen jumped to their feet, not sure whether to shoot back or run for cover. The workers, O'Brien noted with relief, stayed where they were, afraid to move for fear of getting shot.

The gunmen began muttering among themselves. They raked the canyon rim but saw no-one. And then the flap of the smallest tent was pushed back, and Nathan Rocco stepped out into the first sunshine of a new day. His last, if O'Brien had anything to do with it.

He wore his crossed bandoliers and held his Meteor shotgun loosely in his big right hand. He showed no fear, just defiance, as he scanned the canyon rim. He brought his left hand up, slowly, to scratch his stubble-dotted chin. At last, he said, 'Who are you? Show yourself!'

Alvarez came out of the tent behind him, as bronzed and silent as ever. He held a rifle across his narrow chest, his faded brown eyes moving along the rim in search of the intruder. O'Brien saw him stiffen suddenly, and next to him Rocco's stance changed subtly. He guessed that Gleason had stepped into view above.

Rocco stared up at him as the sun began to climb. O'Brien could not read his expression.

''Morning, Rocco,' Gleason shouted down. 'Before you try anything, let me tell you, I have the canyon surrounded, and if you try to make a fight of it, we'll pick you off like rats in a barrel. It's your decision, not mine.'

Rocco did not reply for a while. He glanced briefly at his men, read in their faces their reluctance to fight. They weren't stupid — they knew that Gleason had the advantage of height and, possibly, numbers.

Alternatively, he could be bluffing.

'So you survived the desert, huh, *major*?' Rocco called up. 'You must've been stronger than I gave you credit for.' Gleason made no reply. 'What happened to the others?'

'Oh, they died.'

'So what's the deal, Gleason? What do we get if we surrender?'

'That,' Gleason replied casually, 'is up to Catarina Ortega.'

Rocco laughed. He threw back his head and gave a loud chuckle, then sobered just as quickly. 'That's no deal, and you know it. That bitch'd have me strung up as soon as look at me. You know what I did to her old man, right? I might as well fight.'

'It isn't much of a deal for you, I'll admit, but it's the only one you're going to get,' Gleason replied evenly. 'At least the chances are your men will go free.'

A mumble ran through the gunmen. Rocco threw them a quick glance, defying them to say more, then squinted up at the canyon rim again. He licked his lips. 'You know something, Gleason? I think you're bluffing. No way have you got this place surrounded.'

'Don't try to make me prove it,' Gleason said.

Rocco gave a loud sigh. His shoulders slumped and he looked at the sand at his feet. O'Brien went tense, clutching the Winchester with white fingers. Rocco said, 'All right, all right, you win. You hear me? There won't be no fighting.'

And then he brought the shotgun up, and all hell finally broke loose.

The shotgun roared like approaching thunder. For one split second, Rocco's men were rooted to the spot with surprise. But only for a second. They were professionals, after all. Within a moment they had recovered and began racing for cover, firing hastily at the figures appearing on the rim above them.

Although he had aimed at Gleason, Rocco knew the shotgun would be ineffective at such a range. But that didn't matter. The important thing was that he'd started a fight, under cover of which he might make his escape.

He triggered his second barrel, then broke open the gun and fed in fresh shells from his bandolier. He moved quickly for so big a man, running zigzag towards the remuda.

The canyon filled with the sound of gunfire. One of Rocco's men buckled and fell to the ground, clutching his bullet-torn stomach. Another dropped his gun, grabbing at his wounded arm. Alvarez displayed no emotion at all, just calmly brought his rifle up, took aim and fired.

O'Brien heard a cry from above, then

saw one of the Mexicans, Colquin, hit the canyon floor hard, like a rag doll. His shirt was stained red.

'*Get 'em!*'

O'Brien came up from behind the crates, slapped the stock of the Winchester to his cheek and fired. One of the gunmen went down, dead. Beside him, Jorge triggered a volley of shots. The Mexicans beneath the scaffold did likewise.

This attack threw the gunmen into confusion. Another one hit the ground and lay still. O'Brien flinched as several slugs tore wood from the crates in front of him. He levered another shell into the rifle and fired, cursing when the man he'd aimed for went on running for cover.

Then he caught a movement from the corner of his eye and turned just as Jorge bounced off the veined canyon wall and hit the sand. There was blood on his chest, and he was breathing hard and fast. He looked into O'Brien's eyes and tried to speak, but nothing came out. He continued to stare at O'Brien, even after he was dead.

Rocco shoved through the Mexican workers to get to the remuda. They gave him a wide berth when he showed them the shotgun. The horses stamped and reared, unnerved by the gunfire. There was no time to saddle up, so he quickly chose a strong-looking skewbald, grabbed its mane with his free hand, and swung up onto its back. He stayed low and kicked it viciously in the ribs.

The animal burst out of the remuda and the others, blinded by panic, followed. Suddenly, the canyon was thrown into even greater chaos.

One of the Mexicans under the scaffold, Martinez, came up out of hiding and aimed at Rocco, who was no more than ten feet away. It had to be a quick shot, but Martinez didn't want to miss. Rocco saw him, turned the shotgun his way and took up the pressure on the hair-trigger. The diamond-shaped spray of .00 buckshot almost tore Martinez in half. Then Rocco was gone.

O'Brien saw what had happened and stepped out from behind the crates. He took aim at Rocco, saw a gunman just beyond him about to fire his gun and dived out of the way. The gunman's bullet tore rock chips from the canyon wall. As O'Brien came up again he pulled the trigger and the impact of the bullet ripped the gunman off his feet and hurled him backwards.

Above, Gleason pulled the trigger of his Winchester and cursed when he heard the hammer click on empty. There was no time to reload, so he threw the Winchester down and tore his Colt from its holster. From this position he could see everything happening in the canyon below, but his eyes were on one thing only: Rocco.

The bastard wouldn't escape again, oh no. Gleason's mind filled with a quick succession of images — Morton, Drew, Ruiz, the Mexicans who had died already today, and the white settlers who had been killed by Indians using guns Rocco had supplied years before.

The bastard won't get away this time, he told himself grimly.

He began to race along the canyon rim toward the entrance. Maybe Charro and Lopez would be able to stop him, but then again, maybe not . . .

O'Brien watched Rocco heading for the canyon entrance. Everything hinged on Charro now. Using the wall of horseflesh as cover, O'Brien started toward the gap in the rocks. He took five paces before Alvarez stepped into his path.

The Yaqui's face was lined like an old parchment map. He held his rifle across his chest, and when his eyes met O'Brien's, they did not waver. Then, abruptly, he came forward, swinging the rifle like a club. O'Brien dodged it, stepped back, came in almost immediately, jabbing the barrel of his Winchester at Alvarez' guts. The Yaqui stepped back and O'Brien continued the attack. He thrust out with the Winchester, once, twice, three times, and then Alvarez knocked it away with his own gun, and closed for the kill. He lifted his rifle high, to bring the stock down on O'Brien's head. O'Brien looked into his eyes one last time, then levered a shell into the Winchester and fired. This close, the bullet ripped the Yaqui's guts out in a stringy mess.

Rocco burst through the gap in the rocks and kicked the horse to a gallop. Two things happened very quickly then. Lopez came out of the brush where he had been hiding and triggered a quick shot which hit the horse in the head. It went down in a heap and Rocco was thrown clear. He landed heavily and lay still. Lopez levered another shell into his rifle, stepping forward cautiously.

Just as Charro rose behind him, Rocco rolled onto his stomach and fired the shotgun.

The buckshot blew Lopez away and caught Charro along the left arm. He gave an involuntary cry and went down to one knee. As he pulled his old Dance Brothers .44 from its holster, Rocco came up and tore his knife from its sheath on his belt. It was a thick, wicked looking blade, ten inches long.

He threw it without hardly seeming to take aim. It flew end over end and when it struck Charro's broad chest it sank in almost to the hilt and stayed firm. Charro choked a little and then fell onto his back.

Rocco threw a look around him. The horses were still blocking the canyon entrance. There was no other movement. He fed fresh shells into the shotgun, snapped it shut, then reached down and pulled his knife from Charro's body.

'*Hold it, Rocco!*'

Recognizing Gleason's parade-ground bellow, Rocco whirled, bringing up the shotgun. Gleason was scrabbling down a sandy ridge thirty feet away, his Colt aimed and ready.

Thirty feet . . .

Quickly Rocco worked it out in his mind. The distance was still too great for the shotgun to do much damage, but Gleason might not know that. What did the Army know, anyway?

He fired both barrels.

Gleason dived off to one side to

escape the deadly hail of buckshot. He fell awkwardly on his shoulder and let go of his gun. He grabbed for it but it slid further down the incline.

Rocco threw the empty shotgun to one side and closed fast, the blood-stained knife suddenly appearing in his big, hard fist.

'Come and get it, major, *sir*,' he snarled. 'You've had this coming a *long* time . . . '

He flicked the knife at Gleason, who stumbled backward, still not sure of his footing. Again he cut the air before Gleason's face. He feinted a thrust to the right, and when Gleason dodged it, he changed direction and brought the knife right up into Gleason's gut.

But the former officer went back with the thrust, so the tip of the blade just pricked him. Gleason hit the slope with his back, grabbed a handful of sand and threw it into Rocco's face. The big half-breed gave a yelp and went backward, clawing at his eyes with his free hand. Gleason came up and lashed out with one booted foot. The kick caught Rocco a glancing blow in the balls, and he went back even further.

He recovered quickly, though. As Gleason took another step forward, Rocco straightened to his full height and slashed down with the knife. Gleason cried out as warm blood pumped down his left arm.

Rocco brought the knife back for one last, killing thrust.

'*John! Get back!*'

Gleason's head snapped sideways just as O'Brien came racing out of the canyon. As Rocco turned to face him, Gleason half-fell back out of range of the knife.

Rocco looked at O'Brien for a long time before saying anything. Then, at last, he smiled without humor. 'O'Brien. Well, well, well. Thought you was dead.'

'Not yet,' O'Brien replied evenly. He held the Winchester across his body.

'Not yet,' Rocco repeated hoarsely. 'But soon!'

He threw the knife and dived for Gleason's fallen Colt. As O'Brien dodged the heavy blade, Rocco's fingers clawed in the sand, grabbed the gun, brought it up —

And O'Brien shot him three times.

The first and third bullets tore great red chunks out of his barrel-chest. The second hit right where the two bandoliers crossed his sternum and detonated the shotgun shells resting there.

Nathan Rocco exploded.

The fighting didn't last long after that. By the time they got back to the canyon, it was as good as over. The canyon floor lay littered with bodies. Of Rocco's twenty-one men, twelve were dead, another four wounded. Lamar, one of the two Mexicans who had hidden beneath the scaffold, had taken charge. Together with some of the younger Mexican workers, he had herded the surviving gunmen into the empty remuda.

As O'Brien tied a kerchief around Gleason's arm, the former officer studied them dispassionately. The day was growing warm already, and it was only just seven-thirty.

'All right, listen to me, you men!' he called. 'We're taking you back to Calamajué. It'll be up to *Senorita* Ortega what becomes of you, but I believe she'll be content just to send you packing back across the border. This canyon now belongs to her, and if you ever try to come back to it, you'll be shot on sight. My advice to you is that, when you *do* cross the border, you keep right on going.'

He looked at the twelve laborers. 'As for you, you're free to go home again. Take provisions from the supplies over there, and go back to your families. *Senorita* Ortega will want workers for this mine before long. If you still want jobs, I think you'll find her a better employer than Nathan Rocco.'

To his own battered men, he nodded. 'You did well, all of you. Your friends — *our* friends — who died today will be remembered as heroes.' He looked up at the cloudless sky. There was no sound. Finally, he sighed. 'All right, then, let's move it!'

It was a long haul, coming down out of the Sierra de San Pedro Martir. Even as they rode, O'Brien saw the weather turning, winter approaching.

When they came down into the desert, O'Brien took the opportunity to give Gleason Rocco's shotgun and knife. 'You think Catarina Ortega'll consider these proof enough that we got Rocco?'

Gleason shrugged. 'She ought to. She'll have the word of her most trusted men backing us up.'

Gleason studied O'Brien's profile as he stared out across the desert. There was a definite chill to the air now. 'Why are you giving 'em to me, anyway?' he asked.

O'Brien looked at him and smiled. 'Don't see any point in both of us making the trip all the way back to Calamajué,' he replied casually.

'No, I guess not,' Gleason agreed. 'You're going back to the States?'

'Eventually.'

'I'll look you up sometime.'

'Make sure you do, John.'

Gleason fished in his saddlebag and brought out the bulky envelope Catarina Ortega had given him. 'That's your half of the money.'

O'Brien took it, nodding his thanks.

'When were you thinking of going?' Gleason asked.

By way of reply, O'Brien stuck out his right hand. Gleason raised his eyebrows, then took it. As they shook, Gleason said, '*Vaya con Dios, amigo.*'

O'Brien touched the brim of his hat. '*Hasta luego.*' He studied the Mexicans riding along behind them, keeping watch on the beaten gunmen. '*Adios.*'

Then he rode off, across the desert.

Thirty-five thousand dollars, he thought. That could buy a whole lot of whiskey. A whole lot of whiskey indeed. He thought about whiskey a lot as he crossed the San Felipe desert: it was about the only thing that kept him warm.

It took him six days to cross the desert. By the end of it he decided he could use a hot tub and a week's sleep. It was almost like coming home when he saw the Mission de San Tomas in the distance. He and Gleason would have died if it hadn't been for this place. He would never forget that.

He turned in the saddle to study the Sierra, rising like a misty blue phantom behind him. He thought of Morton and Drew and Ruiz, about Gleason and Rocco and Catarina Ortega. One way or another, it had been an eventful couple of months.

Thoughtfully he peeled five thousand dollars from his bankroll and stuffed it into his pocket. It would keep him going for a while.

When he rode in, the nuns came to greet him like a long-lost son, especially Sister Benedict.

He stayed the night with them, enjoying the feel of clean sheets and the scents of flowers and fruits. The following day he rode on, bound for the border. He took with him their love and best wishes.

He left thirty thousand dollars behind.

We do hope that you have enjoyed reading this large print book.

Did you know that all of our titles are available for purchase?

We publish a wide range of high quality large print books including:
Romances, Mysteries, Classics
General Fiction
Non Fiction and Westerns

Special interest titles available in large print are:
The Little Oxford Dictionary
Music Book, Song Book
Hymn Book, Service Book

Also available from us courtesy of Oxford University Press:
Young Readers' Dictionary
(large print edition)
Young Readers' Thesaurus
(large print edition)

For further information or a free brochure, please contact us at:
Ulverscroft Large Print Books Ltd.,
The Green, Bradgate Road, Anstey,
Leicester, LE7 7FU, England.
Tel: (00 44) **0116 236 4325**
Fax: (00 44) **0116 234 0205**

BLIZZARD JUSTICE

Randolph Vincent

After frostbite crippled the fingers of his gun hand, Isaac Morgan thought his days of chasing desperadoes were over. But when steel-hearted Deputy US Marshal Ambrose Bishop rides into town one winter evening, aiming to bait a trap for a brutal gang which has been terrorizing the border, Morgan's peace is shattered. For after the lawman's scheme misfires, and the miscreants snatch the town judge's beautiful daughter Kitty, Bishop and Morgan must join forces to get her back.

DYNAMITE EXPRESS

Gillian F. Taylor

Sheriff Alec Lawson has come a long way from the Scottish Highlands to Colorado. Life here is never slow as he deals with a kidnapped Chinese woman, moonshine that's turning its consumers blind, and a terrifying incident with an uncoupled locomotive which sees him clinging to the roof of a speeding train car. When a man is found dead out in the wild, Lawson wonders if the witness is telling him the whole truth, and decides to dig a little deeper . . .

HANGING DAY

Rob Hill

Facing the noose after being wrong-fully convicted of his wife's murder, Josh Tillman breaks out of jail. Rather than go on the run, he heads home, determined to prove his innocence and track down the real killer. But he has no evidence or witnesses to back up his story; his father-in-law wants him dead; a corrupt prison guard is pursuing him; and the preacher who speaks out in his defence is held at gunpoint for his trouble . . .